"Ian!" At the bottom finger pressed to h

Then she noticed the blue bulge of the baby holder strapped across his chest. A cherubic creature rested blissfully against him, her eyes closed, lulled by the gentle swell of his breathing.

"You should have called me," Jennifer murmured.

"I tried. You were sound asleep. Nice outfit, by the way." Ian's amused glance made her keenly aware of the silky tank top clinging to her body.

At the rumble of his voice, Rosalie stirred, but snuggled down again with a happy sigh.

How sweet would it be if this child belonged to her, and a deep love united her with this man? whispered a traitorous voice inside Jennifer. Ian was exactly her type, from his lean, rangy body to the ironic tilt of his head. Not to mention the tantalizing hint of the rogue about him.

Dear Reader,

In 2001 California passed the Safely Surrendered Baby Law, popularly known as the safe haven law, to encourage women to leave their newborns in a safe place, such as at a hospital or fire station, rather than abandoning them in a dangerous location. In 2005, the temporary legislation was extended to become permanent.

As a writer, I found myself imagining what if…

What if a young woman who'd lost her own baby has a chance to take one of these surrendered infants home temporarily and falls in love with it? What if she works at a hospital where, for some reason, young mothers in unusual numbers begin leaving their newborns?

Perhaps the circumstance arises because the press misstates the name of the facility, Safe Harbor Medical Center. I pictured the man behind that: a good-looking international reporter who's never given much thought to having a family or child of his own. Suddenly drawn into a situation he inadvertently created, he learns some important lessons about life, himself and, above all, love.

Thus the unlikely love affair between Jennifer and Ian was born. In future books, I hope you'll enjoy the stories of Jennifer's coworkers, their babies, their dreams and their own romantic surprises.

Best wishes,

Jacqueline Diamond

The Would-Be Mommy
JACQUELINE DIAMOND

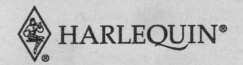

TORONTO • NEW YORK • LONDON
AMSTERDAM • PARIS • SYDNEY • HAMBURG
STOCKHOLM • ATHENS • TOKYO • MILAN • MADRID
PRAGUE • WARSAW • BUDAPEST • AUCKLAND

Recycling programs
for this product may
not exist in your area.

ISBN-13: 978-0-373-75299-7

THE WOULD-BE MOMMY

ABOUT THE AUTHOR

Although her own babies are now young adults, Jacqueline Diamond hasn't forgotten the roller-coaster process of having and nurturing them. A former Associated Press reporter, she maintains a keen interest in medical care and technology, thanks in part to being the daughter of a doctor. To keep tabs on Jackie's more than eighty published novels and free writing tips, please check out www.jacquelinediamond.com. You can write to her at jdiamondfriends@yahoo.com.

Books by Jacqueline Diamond

HARLEQUIN AMERICAN ROMANCE

*Downhome Doctors
†Harmony Circle

For Myrna, who brings sunshine
into my brother's life—and mine!

Chapter One

Everywhere he looked, Ian Martin saw babies. Around the plush hospital lobby, giant photos of babies hung on the walls. Between the designer couches, life-size dolls beamed from their carriages at the throng of local press and small-town dignitaries. Now, if a few Uzi-toting toddlers in camouflage pj's would burst in, *that* might be interesting.

As if he weren't already on infant overload, Ian noticed two women in advanced stages of pregnancy posing for photographs. Presumably they'd both conceived with the high-tech help of the doctors here at Safe Harbor Medical Center, whose six stories of state-of-the-art equipment were detailed on a large wall chart.

Honestly. Didn't these people have anything better to do? He certainly did.

Although Ian had covered wars from Africa to Afghanistan, his editor seemed to think he had a gift for human-interest stories. So, as he was already in Southern California with a free Friday evening, he'd been dispatched to cover the official reopening of this updated, expanded maternity hospital. He'd much rather be digging into the investigation of a federal judge accused of taking bribes, or even poking into the Hollywood divorce scandal that was his secondary reason for descending on the area.

Across the room, he exchanged wry glances with cameraman Pierre Fabray, a coworker from the L.A. bureau of Flash News/Global. With a shrug, Pierre returned his attention to a mom-to-be who, judging by the size of her, must be pregnant with triplets.

Idly, Ian dropped a couple of entry tickets into the raffle box in front of a display of expensive baby furnishings. He'd parted with twenty bucks for them, since the raffle raised money for needy families, the kind that could never otherwise afford these luxurious surroundings. If he won—and Ian had remarkable luck—he planned to donate the gear to charity.

That task accomplished, he gazed around for power players he might be able to prod into saying something provocative. There had to be a story here somewhere. If Ian couldn't find it, he'd stir one up by asking questions somebody didn't want to answer.

First obvious player: hospital administrator Mark Rayburn, a father-knows-best-type obstetrician in his late thirties. Second possibility: a lady from the corporation that owned the hospital. From her spiked heels to her mask of makeup, she looked like she breakfasted on nails and spat them out machine-gun–style at anyone who crossed her.

Neither of them was likely to yield more than an irritable quote or two. Better to locate the inevitable gadfly. There must be a doctor who'd worked at the facility prior to its transformation from a community hospital and who was less than thrilled to see it turned into a haven for the moneyed.

Ian didn't see anyone fitting that description hanging around, shooting his mouth off. He needed assistance, and from what he'd seen of the public relations director, talking to her wouldn't be painful at all.

He located Jennifer Serra outside the auditorium. Dark hair tumbled appealingly from a knot atop her head, and the exotic tilt to her dark eyes intrigued him, as did a hint of sadness that made him wonder what secrets she harbored. But although he was known as much for digging into personalities as for rooting out facts, Ms. Serra wasn't his target tonight. Too bad.

"Mr. Martin!" Her full mouth perked into a smile. "We're almost ready to start the press conference."

"Actually, I'd like to talk to someone first."

"Who?"

"That's what I'm trying to figure out."

Her chin came up. "Anything I can do to help, I'd be glad to."

She shouldn't make tempting offers like that, Ian reflected. On the other hand, being helpful *was* her job. "Who's the most ticked-off doctor at this hospital?"

"I'm sorry?" Her expression turned wary.

"The one who makes trouble." *Kind of like I do.*

She swallowed. He'd made a direct hit, Ian could tell. "We're a team here," she responded gamely.

"And it's your duty to say so. But we both know better." He stretched out an arm and leaned against the wall, deliberately fencing her in. She'd either have to retreat or duck beneath his arm to escape. "A giant corporation buys a community hospital and turns it into a moneymaking machine. That's got to rub somebody the wrong way."

His peripheral vision caught Pierre's approach. Jennifer's face tightened at the sight of the camera, but with what must have been considerable effort, she relaxed into another smile. "If anyone's unhappy, you can hardly expect her to show up at an event like this."

"Her?" So there *was* someone.

Jennifer adjusted the short, fitted jacket she wore over a figure-skimming dress. Ian assumed that bought her a moment to regain control and find the appropriate glib answer. Sure enough, here it came: "Mr. Martin, this is a wonderful facility that brings hope to couples struggling to start a family."

"Of course it does." He filed a mental note to sniff out the disgruntled doctor later, but tonight he needed another angle. "Do you have children?"

"No, not yet." There it was again, that trace of sadness.

"If you ran into trouble having them, could you afford a place like this? Wait—I'm sure you have great insurance. But what about the ordinary infertile woman in Safe Harbor, California? Where is she supposed to go?" While Ian didn't relish making such a pretty lady squirm, the corporation presumably paid her well to cross swords with rascals like him.

Annoyance flared in her eyes. "We're always happy to work out payment plans, and we accept MediCal clients. Plus, we don't just provide fertility treatments. We offer a multitude of services, from routine preventive care to early-stage cancer treatment."

Pierre was angling around, capturing all this for the video service Flash News/Global provided to its clients, along with still-photo images and stories. Personally, Ian wasn't crazy about appearing on video. Digging beneath the surface of the news required an ability to blend into a scene, impossible to do if you became a celebrity. Nevertheless, this was a part of the job, like it or not.

"Is this live?" Jennifer asked Pierre.

"It is now." He turned the camera on Ian. "Go!"

Deep breath. "This is Ian Martin for Flash News/Global, reporting from Safe Harbor, California. We're at a newly remodeled fertility hospital, talking with public relations director Jennifer Serra. We were discussing how this place positively reeks of luxury."

She narrowed her eyes at him in annoyance. Then, as Pierre swung toward her, she said brightly, "Safe Harbor Medical Center offers a full spectrum of services for women and their babies at all economic levels. We specialize in fertility care and high-risk pregnancies, with an emphasis on cutting-edge technology and techniques."

Back to Ian. He seized his chance. "This place may be called Safe Harbor, but just imagine a frightened young woman trying to relinquish her baby under the safe harbor law. If she dared to show up here, I'll bet she'd be whisked out the back door."

That was the advantage video had over writing. You could throw out preposterous ideas and see what kind of reaction you got.

Jennifer took the bait. "We don't whisk anyone out the back door," she snapped. "And that's the safe haven law, not safe harbor. It protects desperate mothers from being charged with abandonment. We want them to bring their newborns to a safe place."

"Safe haven, safe harbor," Ian tossed off. "Are you

saying scared young moms can drop off their babies at Safe Harbor Medical Center? Will they be placed in wealthy homes?"

"They'll be placed in loving homes." A muscle tightened in her neck as Dr. Rayburn and the lady in the power suit came into view.

He decided to push a little harder. "Would *you* take in a surrendered baby?"

"Me personally?"

"Sure. Why not?"

"I love babies." Jennifer swallowed hard. "Every day I walk past our nursery and wish I could hold them all in my arms. But that doesn't mean I could..."

Ignoring a twinge of guilt, Ian persisted. "So if a young mother walked in here right now..."

"I'd do anything I could to help her." Tears sparkled in her eyes. "So would any decent person."

In her face, he read a yearning so profound it twisted his gut. Damn, what wound had he reopened here? They'd gone beyond the usual game between reporter and publicist. Gone straight into her soul.

Live on the Internet.

Ian found his voice again. "Thank you, Jennifer Serra." He squared off with the camera. "This is Ian Martin, reporting from Safe Harbor Medical Center."

Nodding his approval, Pierre killed the feed. Dr. Rayburn and the executive, who'd apparently caught only the last few words, looked pleased.

"Shall we start the conference?" the administrator asked.

"Absolutely." Casting a final glare at Ian, Jennifer headed toward the lobby to corral the rest of the crowd.

Too bad he'd just burned his bridges. It might have been fun getting to know her during the week or so he expected to stay in the L.A. area.

Anyway, she wanted kids, and at her age, which he guessed to be late twenties, was no doubt seeking a guy to nest with. At thirty-four, Ian was strictly a here-today-and-gone-tomorrow kind of guy, and preferred ladies who felt the same.

Yet something about Jennifer haunted him. Perhaps it was the irony that such a beautiful woman seemed so bereft.

Joining the crowd, he wandered into a wood-paneled auditorium with richly upholstered seats, raked flooring and, up front, an impressive display of electronic equipment. Other attendees were still nibbling miniature quiches and bacon-wrapped shrimp hors d'oeuvres, Ian noticed. He wished he'd grabbed a plateful while he'd had the chance.

The auditorium darkened and a slide show began, detailing the facility's remodeling and its shining mission of mercy. There were scenes of beaming parents and earnest doctors in white coats bending over test tubes.

Hold on. Ian straightened at the sight of one slide, which showed a doctor wearing an out-of-place skeptical expression. "The head of our pediatrics department, Dr. Samantha Forrest, works closely with new parents," enthused the narrator. Well, Dr. Forrest, a capable-looking blonde, might care about the couple shown with her, but she clearly didn't enjoy being on camera. What else did she dislike?

Ian trusted his hunches, and he decided to call on Dr.

Forrest soon. Maybe he'd discovered his disaffected troublemaker.

The slide show ended and the lights came up on the TV-star-handsome Dr. Rayburn. Perfectly at ease in front of a microphone, the administrator detailed the new programs, some already in place, others just opening. The emphasis was on the latest medical developments, which, no doubt, were accompanied by breathtakingly high charges.

"Twenty years ago, the success rate for pregnancies with in vitro fertilization was ten to twelve percent," he concluded. "Today, in younger women, we can expect to achieve a sixty to seventy percent rate. With older women, the rates are also much higher than they used to be, and this is just the beginning of the adventure. Now I'm happy to take questions."

Ian didn't bother to make notes as other reporters threw out inquiries.

"Delivering a baby is the most wonderful feeling in the world." Dr. Rayburn responded to one question with passionate commitment. Where had the corporation discovered this guy—Hollywood central casting?

Ian flipped through the press kit an assistant had handed him earlier. In Dr. Rayburn's bio, he saw no mention of a wife or children. If delivering a baby was so fabulous, why hadn't the great doctor produced any of his own?

That seemed too personal to ask in front of a crowd, though. Instead, Ian chose the ever-popular topic of multiple births. "Is there a limit on how many embryos you implant in a woman?" he demanded without waiting to be called out.

"We implant two or three embryos at most," the administrator responded. "We try to avoid multiple births that can endanger the health of mothers and babies. Now, let's hear from Medical Center Management vice president Chandra Yashimoto."

The lady exec stepped forward to contribute a few words about the pride her company, based in Louisville, Kentucky, took in this new facility. The press kit listed neither an M.D. nor an R.N. after her name.

Ms. Yashimoto yielded the microphone to Jennifer.

"I hope you'll all stick around and enjoy the refreshments," she said, her voice pleasingly husky. "Also, we'll be announcing the winner of our baby bonanza raffle shortly. Furniture, clothes, all the gear you need for a great start."

After a breath, she plunged into an obviously prepared wrap-up. "Although the hospital has remained open during remodeling, our staff endured a lot of disruption over the summer. We were aiming for a September opening, and here we are, right on track. I now officially declare our doors open. Thank you all for joining us."

A smattering of applause followed. As the audience got to its feet, Ian tried to figure out his next move. Technically, he'd done his job, providing Pierre with video and amassing enough material to write an article. A routine one, but Flash News/Global would move it out, since weekends tended to be slow for news without courts and legislatures in session.

All the same, Ian hated writing forgettable pieces. He craved an angle.

A sudden stir caught his attention. Willa Lightner, the

middle-aged PR assistant who'd been distributing press kits earlier, had entered from the hall and was excusing her way up the center aisle toward Jennifer. The two met, conferred and hurried out together.

Something was up. Might be nothing more than a knocked-over punch bowl, but, his curiosity aroused, Ian strode in their wake.

He trailed them around a bend and into an alcove where half a dozen people had gathered. It took a moment to identify the object of their interest.

A young woman stood with her back against the wall, her arms encircling a blanket-wrapped bundle. Loose brown hair cascaded around a face in which determination warred with fear. In contrast to the moms-to-be Ian had seen earlier, she wore a threadbare smock and flip-flops. Definitely not part of the hospital's show and tell program.

He took out his notebook and looked around. Pierre was headed his way. Excellent.

In front of him, Jennifer parted the small group of onlookers. "Hi. I'm the public relations director. Can I help you?"

The young woman thrust the bundle into her arms. "I know who you are, Mrs. Serra. I just saw you on the Internet." Her voice trembled. "You said you love babies and you'd give them a home. Well, I want you to adopt mine."

For a thunderstruck moment, nobody moved. Except Ian, who made quick notes on his pad.

He'd found his story at last.

Chapter Two

Landing this job at Safe Harbor six months ago had been an excellent career move for Jennifer and a major salary increase over her last position. So what if the constant presence of pregnant women reminded her of the baby she'd lost, the one she'd never dared tell anyone about?

Setting up Safe Harbor's official opening, arranging the displays of baby photos and the raffle of baby goods, had squeezed her spirits again and again. But she'd grown used to it. Toughened up.

Or so she'd thought until that Flash News/Global reporter threw her a curveball. *Do you have children?* Not an unusual question—people often asked it innocently enough—but something about his half-teasing expression had taken her unawares.

Well, she'd just been caught off guard again, by a tiny infant swaddled in pink. And by the sight of the young mother with red-rimmed eyes and a cracked lower lip. *That might have been me, a dozen years ago.* Except that Jennifer's baby hadn't survived long enough to be born.

When the mother thrust the bundle at her, Jennifer's arms closed around it instinctively. The scent of talcum powder burst into her brain, and the subtle snuggling as the tiny girl adjusted to her grasp sent tremors through her nervous system. She could hardly tear her gaze from the angelic blue eyes and bow-shaped mouth.

For a moment, Jennifer couldn't speak. It didn't matter, because the young woman was talking again.

"Her name's Rosalie. I can't keep her. I want you to be her mother now." Tearfully, the mother edged away.

"Wait. What's your name?" Jennifer blurted.

"Sunny." Another move toward the exit.

"You can't leave yet." Anxiously, Jennifer noticed the reporter, Ian, closing in, along with his cameraman and a news team from a local TV station.

"I have to go." Sunny shielded her face protectively and, to their credit, the camera operators focused on the baby instead.

With relief, Jennifer saw a familiar face emerge from the crowd and approach the young mother. "Hi. I'm the hospital's staff attorney," Tony Franco told Sunny gently. "I need you to sign papers to release her. We just have to make sure she really belongs to you and to get a little medical background. Can you come with me?"

"I'll wait here." Sunny folded her arms, clearly unwilling to go anywhere with anyone.

Tony appeared to debate with himself, but he had little choice. "Okay, I'll go grab the forms. Two minutes, I promise." He headed off at a lope.

Still averting her face from the press, Sunny peered desperately at Jennifer. "You'll take her yourself, right?"

She had to be sensible. "We'll find a home for her."

"Not just any home!" Panic edged the young woman's voice. "You said on the Internet that you'd raise her."

Jennifer was sure she hadn't quite said *that*. But she'd learned in public relations that people often misinterpreted what they heard according to their own needs. "I doubt county Social Services will allow it. But there are lots of loving parents waiting."

Sunny touched Jennifer's sleeve. "Please. I'd feel so much better if I knew she was with you."

As if on cue, Rosalie let out a contented sigh that cut right through Jennifer's resistance. If only…

Still, there were rules about adoptions, and taking in a newborn would be an incredible responsibility. More than that, Jennifer wasn't even remotely prepared emotionally. To give her heart, only to risk losing the baby again if the authorities decreed otherwise… "I'll make sure she finds the right family. That's the best I can do."

Sunny appeared to be wavering, on the point of giving in. Good. She had to see reason.

Then Ian Martin addressed Jennifer. "Poor kid. She's already being abandoned once. Don't tell me you're going to abandon her again."

If she hadn't had her arms full, Jennifer would have been tempted to punch him. What did a shallow reporter—who'd probably been hired mainly for his dark blond good looks—know about raising a child, anyway?

"No one's abandoning anyone," she replied fiercely.

"What do you call it when you hand that little cutie over to a social worker?" He quirked an eyebrow, obviously enjoying the situation.

"You're out of line," Jennifer told him. "This isn't a game, Mr. Martin. There are real people's futures at stake here."

He blinked as if she'd slapped him. Slapped him

awake from his self-absorption for a second, anyway. She had no doubt he'd slip right into it again soon, but with luck, by then he'd be haring after some other hapless target.

Dr. Rayburn joined the group, his forehead creased with concern. Beside him, Chandra Yashimoto stared disapprovingly at the scene.

Painfully aware of the cameras trained on them, Jennifer realized she had to handle the situation before it turned into a media circus. "This is a private matter and we'd appreciate your respecting that," she told the press.

No one stirred. Chandra cleared her throat, obviously expecting the PR director to take further action.

Oh, for a distraction. The raffle! "Over the past few months we've sold enough tickets to collect roughly ten thousand dollars for charity," Jennifer informed the crowd. "If you'll follow my assistant, Mrs. Lightner, to the baby furnishings display, she's going to draw the name of the winner. Afterward, I'll be happy to take everyone on a tour of our facilities."

Willa waved one hand eagerly. "This way, everybody! You shouldn't miss this." She linked arms with the startled Ian and tugged him forward. "Since you're clearly devoted to children's welfare, Mr. Martin, I'm sure you'll tell the world about the winner and all the money we raised." She drew him and the other observers away with a combination of briskness and persuasion. You could tell she was the parent of teenagers, Jennifer mused.

When they were gone, she turned to Dr. Rayburn. "I'm sorry for letting things get out of hand."

"Not your fault," he said.

Ms. Yashimoto scowled. "This is awkward."

"Who're you?" demanded Sunny, who'd taken refuge behind Dr. Rayburn. "Don't let *her* take my baby. She looks like she eats them for breakfast."

Biting down on a smile, Jennifer made introductions. "I have two grandchildren," Ms. Yashimoto informed the young mother. "For your information, I haven't eaten either of them yet."

Sunny looked unconvinced.

Tony returned with the paperwork and some news. He'd called the county child welfare agency and learned that, due to a staffing shortage, no one would be available to pick up the baby until Monday.

"We could accommodate her in the nursery," Dr. Rayburn suggested.

A tear etched a path down Sunny's cheek. "I can't leave her alone. Who'll hold her when she cries?"

Jennifer couldn't bear the thought, either. "I suppose I could take her for the weekend," she said. "If you really want me to."

The young mom sniffled. "Thank you. You'll fall in love with her. I know you will."

Jennifer brushed a kiss across the baby's soft cheek. "And I'll stay on top of things until she's placed. I promise."

"Okay. I trust you." Sunny snatched Tony's pen and filled in the papers. She didn't do a very thorough job, but apparently it passed muster with the attorney. "Have a nice life," she whispered to her daughter. "Be good so the nice lady loves you." Tears streaming, she rushed away.

Jennifer longed to call after her and suggest she seek counseling. Too late. The young mom was gone.

From the lobby, a burst of applause indicated the raffle winner had been announced. And Ms. Yashimoto's glare brought home the point that Jennifer ought to be tending to her duties, not standing there holding a baby.

"I'll take the baby up to the nursery for an exam." Nurse Lori Ross, who'd hung back during the incident, came to Jennifer's side. A good friend, she was a welcome sight.

"That would be wonderful. I'll pick her up in about an hour," Jennifer said gratefully.

"I'll arrange for diapers and formula, too," Lori promised. "If you like, I could come over later and show you how to use them."

Jennifer chuckled. "I used to babysit. But thanks."

"See you later." The nurse took the infant. Cool air rushed in where Rosalie had warmed Jennifer's arms.

"I'll get you a loaner car seat," Tony added.

"Thanks."

"Absolutely," said Ms. Yashimoto. "Think of the liability if they had an accident!" She cleared her throat. "And of course, we don't want anyone to get hurt."

As the others departed, Jennifer took a moment to settle her racing thoughts. Sunny's pleading expression…that darling baby… How on earth could she have resisted?

By using your common sense, that's how.

Babies didn't stay babies. They grew into toddlers, and little girls, and then teenagers who required guidance and stability. They deserved two parents, or at least a mother who'd planned for them. Definitely not a mom who'd had an infant thrust into her arms because of a silly misunderstanding.

But this was only for the weekend. That was all she'd promised, and all she could reasonably provide.

Straightening her shoulders, Jennifer headed for the lobby. From the buzz of voices, she gathered that people were scattering, which meant she'd better hurry and round up those interested in a tour.

Entering, she was pleased to see that Willa had cornered Ian. *Keep that man busy.* Just the sight of him frayed Jennifer's temper.

Usually, she didn't let reporters bother her, but he was uncommonly pesky and smug. And too much like the daredevils she used to find irresistible, before she grew up the hard way.

"Over here for the tour!" Jennifer called. "I promise, if anyone gets bored, I won't be offended if you hop on the nearest elevator. But you won't want to miss seeing our nurseries."

"More than one?" inquired a city councilwoman.

"We have nurseries providing several levels of care, depending on babies' needs," Jennifer explained. "Also, did I mention there's a helicopter pad on our roof?"

"I'm hooked," said a man she recognized as the police chief. "Count me in."

A cheerful group assembled. Jennifer was leading them to the main elevators when she spotted Ian's cameraman, a trendy urban type with a shaved head and a tattoo peeking above his T-shirt, cutting across the lobby in their direction. Well, she could hardly object, since he *was* a member of the press.

And here came Ian, his long legs making short work of the distance. What a striking contrast to his associate: stylishly cut hair, careless but expensive black jacket, and a tie loosened just enough to tempt a woman to give it a tug.

Some other woman.

In the elevator, Jennifer wished she weren't keenly aware of Ian's sophisticated aftershave. She must have noticed it before, subliminally, because she identified it with him instantly.

"Congratulations," the councilwoman told him.

On what? Jennifer was about to ask when the doors opened on the third floor. She had to step out and shepherd everyone to the labor and delivery areas. From there, they proceeded to the nurseries.

The hospital wasn't full, thanks to the low profile it had maintained during renovations, but there were still plenty of babies visible through the nursery windows. As Jennifer detailed the state-of-the art equipment, a sense of calm replaced her earlier agitation.

She knew her job. And she knew this hospital. Whatever curveballs Ian Martin decided to throw, she could field them.

She didn't have long to wait. A few minutes later, when she pointed out the on-call sleeping rooms for staff, Ian asked whether Safe Harbor doctors indulged in sexual shenanigans like the characters on TV doctor shows.

"Absolutely not. That would be unprofessional," Jennifer responded coolly.

He grinned. Enjoyed provoking her, obviously. Well, his wire service didn't often cover events in such a small town, so with luck she wouldn't have to see him again.

Continuing the tour, she showed off a gleaming lab, an operating room, a Wi-Fi-equipped patient lounge and some of the overnight facilities for families. Several visitors commented on the convenience of pharmacies on every floor and a cafeteria with an on-site chef from 6:00 a.m. to 10:00 p.m.

"Do they serve vegetarian food?" the council-woman inquired.

"Vegetarian *and* vegan," Jennifer replied. "We offer a diabetic menu, as well."

After touring the rooftop helicopter pad, they returned to the lobby. Her small group disbanded, except for Ian.

Just her luck.

"Is there anything else you need?" For heaven's sake, how much attention did this man expect when she was eager to get upstairs to Rosalie?

"I was wondering where the baby will sleep tonight." Penetrating blue eyes caught hers.

Without the camera aimed at him, surely he didn't plan any more lectures about abandonment. "At my place," she said tightly.

"In your bed?"

Of all the nerve! "You've just overstepped your bounds, so I'll say good-night."

"Wait!" He caught her elbow, sending an unwelcome flare of heat through Jennifer's arm. "That came out wrong."

"Exactly what would have been the right way for it to come out?" She pulled her arm free.

He cocked his well-shaped head—the man was attractive, and knew it—and indicated the baby furniture on the far side of the lobby. "Guess you missed the excitement. I'm the big winner."

Him? That explained the councilwoman's congratulations, as well as his long conversation with Willa,

Jennifer supposed. "If you'll tell us where to deliver it, we'll be happy to."

He watched her as if waiting for a punch line. "We can deliver it ourselves in Pierre's van."

"Wonderful. If you're donating it to charity, I'll give you credit in our press release." *Now go away.*

"Guess I'm not making myself clear."

"There's more?" She steeled herself to keep from backing away.

"You really don't like me, do you." The words came out more rueful than offended.

"It's my job to be nice to you." That was the most diplomacy she could manage at the moment.

"You hate me that much, huh?"

"I think you're a…" Jennifer took a deep breath and slowly counted to three. "A reporter doing his job."

"What I've been trying to say, rather clumsily, is that Pierre and I will haul the baby furniture over to your place. I'm assuming you don't have a crib and a stroller and whatever else is in that lot."

A changing table, baby sheets, receiving blankets, a diaper stacker and plenty more… Jennifer could recite the inventory by heart, having arranged with the stores that had donated it. She conceded that she'd misjudged Ian's intentions. "Thank you. I'm not sure I need all that for two days, though."

"Give it to charity when you're finished," he said.

"You really don't need to—"

"How about letting me act like a nice guy for a change? I'd say I owe you a favor."

He certainly did. If it weren't for him, Jennifer wouldn't be in this bind. Still, she *had* been curt.

"I'd appreciate borrowing the baby equipment," she conceded. "But anything that happens after we leave the medical center is off the record. No videos, no quotes."

"Done." He waved to Pierre. "How far do you live?"

"Less than a mile." Close enough to walk to work occasionally, although she didn't see any reason to mention that. Despite Ian's cooperative attitude, Jennifer still didn't trust the man. She intended to tell him as little as possible.

About anything.

Chapter Three

"I could video the outside of her building. A condo complex, she said?" Pierre mused as he piloted the van along a side street. "Maybe I'll accidentally-on-purpose catch her carrying the baby inside."

Ian dragged his gaze off the compact car they were trailing, which from this height looked awfully fragile to protect a woman and a baby. "I gave my word."

"Ridiculous," his companion muttered. "We're newsmen, for Pete's sake."

"Ever heard of being off duty?"

"This from a man reputed to have taken a bullet in his shoulder in Baghdad, wrapped it in a scarf and finished his interview?"

"Greatly exaggerated." Or so he preferred for people to think.

"If we aren't working, what're we doing here?" grumbled the cameraman.

"A good deed."

"What's that?"

Ian laughed. "Mr. Hard Nose."

"Mr. Been in L.A. so long I can tell the gangs apart

by their tattoos," Pierre countered. "People in Safe Harbor have it easy. Big deal, she has to take care of a baby for a few days. It's a story, man."

"I promised her."

"I didn't."

"Cross me and I can find a thousand ways to make your life miserable while I'm in town."

"Threats, threats." Despite his grumbling, Pierre was clearly acquiescing. This wasn't *that* big a story.

In truth, Ian wasn't sure why he felt determined to help Jennifer. Guilt? Attraction? Curiosity?

Her remark had jolted him. *This isn't a game. There are real people's futures at stake.* Real people's futures were at stake in Baghdad, too. And Rome, and Beijing and other places he'd covered. But until now he'd never provoked a turn of events through his own needling.

Still, the young woman—Sunny—would have left the baby somewhere. At least the video had guided her to this cushy hospital and softhearted Jennifer Serra.

He didn't owe anybody anything. Drop off the furniture, bid the lady sayonara and go toss back a few cold beers. That was the ticket. Yet his spirits sank at the prospect of sitting in yet another bar like a hundred others around the globe, except for the California smokeless air and transfat-free taco chips.

Why was he worrying about this stuff, anyway? Must be due to the approach next month of his thirty-fifth birthday. That made a man stop and take stock. For about five minutes, Ian hoped.

The car pulled to the curb in front of a stucco building. Through the compact's window, Jennifer waved at the van to halt behind her.

"Nice place," Pierre muttered.

Ian noted a planter overflowing with petunias and, in a nearby unit, a greenhouse window filled with herbs. "Cozy," he agreed.

"Typical Orange County." The camera operator made the name sound like an insult.

"Where exactly do *you* live?" Although they worked together whenever Ian was in L.A., he didn't know Pierre all that well.

"A den of iniquity in Hollywood."

"Sounds charming." Ian pushed open his door.

"The rats like it."

"You have pet rats?"

The man chuckled. "Okay, no rats. But no greenhouse windows, either."

Jennifer awaited them on the sidewalk, the baby tucked into a stroller and her foot tapping impatiently. She wasted no time heading into her two-story unit, where, naturally, the baby furniture went upstairs, into an empty bedroom.

Ian and Pierre hauled in the changing table, crib and bureau. How could one little kid require this much stuff? At least it had all been assembled prior to being put on display. If not, Ian conceded, he'd probably have felt obligated to put them together.

At last they wedged their final load—a chest of baby clothes, shoes, toys and books—into a corner of the bedroom. According to Ian's watch, it was only a little past nine.

"Still early enough to keep my pressing engagement," Pierre said as they descended.

"You have a pressing engagement?"

"I always have a pressing engagement," he replied coolly. "How about you?"

"Only to file my story." While it might be Friday night here, morning was dawning on the other side of the globe, and viewers of the baby-surrender video would be eager for more details.

On the living-room couch, Jennifer sat feeding the baby a bottle. Idly, Ian noted the colorful decor: lemony walls, red-checked curtains and a splash of green from hanging plants. Plus, of course, the blue-and-pink portable bassinet and baby gear strewn across the coffee table.

"You okay?" he asked.

Jennifer nodded wearily. "I appreciate everything you've done."

"No problem. You sure you're fine by yourself?" He had no idea where this surge of protectiveness came from.

Tendrils of her once-artful hairstyle straggled down her cheeks as she nodded, and then she paused. "Oh!"

The single syllable froze him in the doorway. "Yes?"

From her pocket, she produced a set of keys. "If I leave my car on the street, I'll get a ticket. Would you mind moving it? The parking space is in the carport around back, with my unit number."

The exhaustion in Jennifer's voice tugged at Ian. She'd worked hard today, and she no doubt faced a wakeful night due to his meddling. "No problem."

"Also, Dr. Rayburn insisted I take some of the left-overs from the reception," she added. "If you could bring those in, I'd really appreciate it."

"Glad to." He caught the keys in midair and stepped outside.

"Man, hurry it up, will you?" Pierre growled.

"I think I'll stick around awhile," he said as they went down the walkway. "You go on without me."

"You sure?"

"Might get a few more quotes for my story." That made a convincing explanation. It could turn out to be the truth, if Jennifer agreed. Mostly, though, he wanted to make sure she got settled properly.

"You'll have to walk back to your car," Pierre warned.

Right. He'd left it at the hospital. "Only a mile," Ian pointed out. In most places in the world, people thought nothing of hiking that distance.

"See you Monday. Or sooner, if anything breaks."

"You bet."

Jennifer's car started easily, and Ian found the parking space with no trouble. From the trunk, he removed two large caterer's boxes that, judging by the weight, held enough food for a small village. The scents of cheese and bacon reminded him that he'd forgotten to eat earlier.

He hoped she planned to share.

Swinging down a pathway through the landscaped courtyard, Ian registered the low chatter of TV sets, an aria from *La Bohème* soaring out of an upstairs window and, from somewhere, a burst of male and female laughter. The sweet scent of jasmine drifted to him on a mild September breeze. For a fleeting moment, he imagined himself living in a refuge like this, returning home each night to comfortable furniture and a familiar, welcoming smile….

If he reacted this way to turning thirty-five, he shuddered to think what tricks his mind might play at forty. Nope, his imagination didn't stretch that far.

After a sharp knock, he let himself into Jennifer's unit. She hadn't moved from the couch, where she and the baby appeared on the verge of falling asleep.

"Sorry to interrupt." He hefted the boxes. "Would you like me to tuck these in the fridge?"

"Actually, I'm starving." Gently, she lifted the infant and positioned her in the bassinet. "I was too busy to eat earlier."

"I missed dinner myself." As a consequence of an unpredictable schedule and frequent shifts of time zone, Ian rarely kept track of meals.

"You realize those are fighting words to a woman?" Jennifer teased. "I can't let a man leave my home hungry." So she had a domestic side. That was hard to resist in his present mood.

When she lifted one of the white boxes from his hands, Ian registered that she just reached his shoulder. The perfect height for dancing, not that they were ever likely to. Or for gathering close and kissing, which seemed even less likely. Damn it.

He followed her into an airy kitchen enlivened by a yellow-and-white-checked tablecloth and a gleaming wood floor. He set his box beside hers on the counter. "Did you decorate this place yourself?"

"Every stroke of paint and stick of furniture." She lifted blue plates from a cabinet. "I grew up in dingy rentals. Until I was over eighteen, I didn't realize you could buy cookware any place but Goodwill."

He'd assumed she came from a posh environment like the one where she worked. "Making up for lost time?"

"With a vengeance." She opened catering boxes to reveal hors d'oeuvres ranging from egg rolls to meatballs, plus the quiches and bacon-wrapped shrimp he'd spotted previously. "I could heat this if you like."

"Cold is fine with me." If he'd been finicky about food, he wouldn't have lasted long at his job. "Do you have any cayenne pepper?"

"You like your food spicy, I take it."

"Kind of an addiction."

Jennifer fetched a small shaker from the spice rack. "Wine?" she asked as he heaped up a plate. "I have an open bottle of merlot."

"Perfect. Thanks." Ian couldn't recall the last time he'd eaten a leisurely meal in a woman's kitchen. Not since he last visited his sister.

"You live in L.A.?" Jennifer asked as she set down his glass. Beneath a hanging lamp, the wine glowed in the leaded, hand-cut crystal.

"Me?" Sometimes Ian forgot that he didn't have *nomad* printed on his forehead. "I don't exactly live anywhere. My news agency is based in Brussels." In case her geography was vague, he added, "That's in Belgium."

"I'm aware of that."

"Some people assume it's in the Netherlands or France."

"Or in the middle of a field of sprouts?"

"That, too."

She downed a bite of food before continuing. "If you don't have a home, where do you store your personal records and stuff you want to keep?"

"In my sister's attic." He dug into the meatballs. "These are great. I approve of your caterer."

"Finding the best vendors is part of my job." She sipped her wine. "Where does your sister live?"

"In Brussels. She's married to my editor. I made the mistake of introducing them. Well, not a mistake, since they're happy, but it's a bit odd taking orders from my brother-in-law." Although they didn't always see eye to eye, he liked Viktor.

"Older or younger sister?"

"Same age. We're twins."

"That's unusual."

"Not for us."

She chuckled. "You grew up in Europe?" The note of wonder in her voice reminded him that many people considered his upbringing exotic.

"I was born in a very unromantic spot known as Buffalo, New York," Ian said. "Dad was in the import-export business, so we served time in Italy, France and Shanghai."

Jennifer regarded him wistfully. "I've always wanted to travel."

"We lived in some beautiful places," Ian conceded. "It was hard constantly leaving friends behind, though." He rounded off with the obligatory disclosure, "I went to college in New York City. Columbia University. Journalism."

"That's impressive," Jennifer murmured.

"What about you?"

"Cal State Fullerton. Communications."

Ian had meant the rest of her background, not so much her alma mater. "Did you grow up around here?"

"Palm Highlands," she said. "Out in the desert. About the most boring place on the planet, unless you're fascinated by biker bars, run-down diners and motels with half the lights burned out in the Vacancy sign."

"I've seen worse."

"In France and Italy?"

"Afghanistan. Iraq. Somalia." As he reeled off the names, Ian tried to blot the images of bombed-out buildings, the smell of smoke, the sound of wailing. Sitting in this comfortable kitchen, it was hard to recall why he'd been so eager to get back there.

"What on earth brings you to Safe Harbor?"

"My brother-in-law has this crazy idea that my real gift is human-interest stories."

"Well, you're pushy and ingratiating," she teased. "I suppose that counts for something." After scooting her chair back, she went into the living room to check on the baby. On her way back, she stopped at the counter.

"Pushy and ingratiating," Ian repeated. "You're blunt after a glass of wine. What happens after two glasses?"

"I try not to find out." She refilled her plate. "There are cheesecake bites and brownies, or didn't you notice?"

Amazingly, he'd missed them. "Count me in."

They capped off the meal with a cup of decaf. Usually Ian would have stuck to wine or something stronger, but he had a long drive ahead.

Across from him, Jennifer stretched stocking-clad feet onto an empty chair and licked a cheesecake crumb from her finger. Nice mouth, Ian noted once again. Under other circumstances, he might consider finding out how it felt beneath his. Or perhaps, if their moods mellowed even further…

"What comes next?" she asked.

His body responded instinctively to the possibilities. He could almost feel her heat against him, her sweet yielding. "Next?"

"Yes." Her eyes widened as she caught his expression. "I didn't mean that!"

Ian nearly choked on his coffee. "I'm sorry."

A blush spread across her cheeks. "Are you all right?"

"Hold the Heimlich. I'm fine." He stifled his coughing with another swallow. "Repeat the question, would you? I think I've returned to my right mind."

"I meant, now that you've wowed your viewers on the Internet, where do you jet off to?"

"First I have to write tonight's story. Then I've got a corrupt judge to investigate. And a Hollywood scandal, which isn't serious, but for some reason people like to read about that."

"You said something earlier about war zones." An eyebrow arched skeptically. "And here I took you for just another pretty face in front of the camera."

That was truly what she'd thought of him? "Thanks for the backhanded compliment. Always glad to be considered pretty." He rubbed his jaw ruefully, and noted a bristly hint of stubble. "Would a beard improve my image?"

Her toes twitched. "No, but another round of cheesecake might. Men always look better when I'm on sugar overload."

"At your service." He transferred the platter of desserts to the table. "The truth is, covering the hospital debut was a way to kill a slow evening."

"Well, smack me in the ego," she said drily.

If he weren't careful, he might start to like this woman more than he should, Ian mused. When in doubt, he did what he always did: got down to business. "Since I still have a story to write, is it okay if I mention that baby Rosalie is happily settled with you for the weekend? Inquiring minds will want to know."

"Just don't print my address." Jennifer polished off another brownie. "That's my limit, by the way. Take the rest of them with you. Brain food."

"Dessert is brain food?"

"Late-night energy boost," she explained.

Being around her provided all the energy boost Ian needed, but he had better judgment than to mention *that*. "I'll take half in case you get hungry again. By the way, if my schedule permits, I might drop by the hospital next week for a follow-up on the baby."

"If you're too busy, you can always send that endearing cameraman. What's his name—Pierre? If he ever gets laid off, I hope he'll consider a second career as a hospitality hostess. It's a shame for all that charm to go to waste."

Lucky that Ian had finished his coffee or he'd have choked on it again. "You saw right through his surly facade."

"Right into his surly heart."

Digging into his pocket, he produced a business card. "Here's my number. Call me if you find out Rosalie's the secret love child of a movie star. Or if you need someone to run out for diapers and formula this weekend. I'm staying in L.A., but I like driving." Although he wasn't sure why he made the offer, he meant it.

"If an earthquake hit right now, we probably have enough diapers and formula to last for weeks." She glanced at the card. "What does the *R* in your middle initial stand for?"

"Rascal," he said.

"Not Rumormonger?"

"Robert, actually." Getting to his feet, he did his best to brush a ridiculously large amount of crumbs into a paper napkin.

"That gives you three first names," Jennifer observed lazily, as if feeling the effects of the wine. "Ian Robert Martin. Is your twin sister by any chance named Ina?"

"Close. Anni."

"Anni Roberta Martin?"

"You're wicked," he said. "No. And her last name is now DeJong."

"Nice to have met you, Ian Robert Martin," Jennifer said. "The wastebasket's under the sink."

As he disposed of the napkin, it occurred to him that she hadn't provided *her* cell number. Then he recalled seeing it on a press release. The woman must live and breathe her work. A lot like he did. "Sleep well."

"I'll try."

On his way out, Ian paused by the bassinet. Although Rosalie's lids were shut, her little mouth appeared to be sucking, and she twitched. Dreaming, he thought, and wondered what babies dreamed of.

After making sure the door locked behind him, he set out toward the hospital. He relished the cool night air and the chance to think.

Tonight, for the space of a few hours, Ian had simply lived in the moment and enjoyed talking to a woman more than he had in years. He liked this place. He could understand how it might lure a man.

But he doubted he'd return, except for work. Over the years, he'd seen too many reporters go off track. They'd traded promising careers and opportunities to change the world for a peaceable life and the mediocrity that came with it.

That was not going to happen to Ian Robert Martin. For him, Safe Harbor could never be more than a temporary port.

Chapter Four

Twice that night, Jennifer awoke and went down the hall to the baby's room. Each time, Rosalie drained her bottle and cuddled happily with her new, temporary mom in the borrowed rocking chair.

What circumstances had led to this birth? Why had Sunny felt obliged to give her up? Too bad Jennifer hadn't had a chance to talk privately with the young mother.

At seventeen, Jennifer hadn't been certain she'd be able to keep her own baby, but she would have tried. Had her son lived, he'd be twelve now, junior-high age. What would he be like? Would he be here, or growing up with an adoptive family?

It was useless to agonize over the past. Equally futile to imagine, as Jennifer did in these sleepy, vulnerable moments, that she might try to adopt Rosalie. Following impulses led to disappointment and sometimes actual harm. No one knew that better than she did.

Still, she was glad she'd yielded to Sunny's urgent request, for as long as it lasted. Often in the middle of the night like this, loneliness squeezed Jennifer's heart. Not tonight. For this brief reprieve, she had a baby to hold. And she was grateful.

This evening, too, she'd felt painful stirrings while she was around Ian Martin. He was exactly the kind of man that used to attract her—intense, amusing, volatile. Men like that always let her down, though. And they always would, if she gave them the chance.

So she wouldn't.

Jennifer returned the baby to the crib. She had a job she loved, along with two very dear new friends. And she'd better get to bed so she didn't oversleep and miss their regular Saturday outing.

At nine o'clock the next morning, having polished off the remaining brownies and cheesecake bites, she threw on jeans, a tank top and matching sweater and tucked Rosalie into the borrowed stroller. In front of the complex, they found Lori waiting, and together set out on their power walk.

"How'd the baby do last night?" The nurse peered into the carriage as they strode. "How about you? I heard the reporter loaned you the furniture he won. Did that go all right? He didn't stay too late, did he? You look well rested."

Although accustomed to her friend's bubbly nature, Jennifer rarely saw her this chatty. "It was fine. And what did you OD on this morning?"

"Jared came over late last night. He just left a few minutes ago." That explained the flyaway state of Lori's reddish-brown hair.

She and Jared Sellers, a staff neonatologist, had been dating for several months. Although hospital policy discouraged courtships at work, there were no rules against dating in one's private life. Besides, technically the two didn't work together. Lori assisted Mark Rayburn with his infertility patients, while Jared treated newborns. In fact, he was the doctor who'd examined Rosalie last night.

At the hiking trail, they found Samantha Forrest jogging in place as she awaited them. The pediatrician might be a few years older than Lori and Jennifer, but she kept in tip-top shape. "Whose baby is that?" she asked, angling for a better look.

"You didn't see us on the Internet?" Jennifer joked. "For all I know, it made the eleven o'clock news, as well." Ian hadn't been the only reporter present.

"What made the news?" Samantha asked as they set out abreast. Luckily, no one was around to object to them blocking the path.

Jennifer explained about the evening's events, with Lori throwing in excited comments. Her enthusiasm seemed excessive, since the nurse claimed not to be crazy about babies. The oldest of six girls, Lori had helped raise her younger siblings, and that, she'd declared, was all the parenting she ever cared to provide.

"She relinquished the baby in front of the cameras?" Samantha queried as they passed a bougainvillea-draped wall that obscured their view of expensive bluff-top homes. "I'll bet Mark and that executive gave her the bum's rush."

Sam made no secret of her dissatisfaction with the hospital administration. She'd risen to director of pediatrics a few years ago when the facility served many poor families. It still accepted maternity patients on a sliding scale, but a clinic offering low-cost care had been closed.

"Dr. Rayburn was very supportive," Jennifer corrected.

"And Ms. Yashimoto?"

"The less said, the better." She adjusted the stroller's hood to keep the sunlight off Rosalie's face. The baby returned her gaze contentedly.

Don't get too attached, sweetheart. I can't keep you, she thought, and then wondered if she was aiming that reminder at the baby or at herself.

"Did you tell Sam about the reporter who won the contest? He's cute," Lori prompted, and hurried on to describe Ian's rangy good looks and the generous loan of his winnings. Jennifer hardly had a chance to say anything, which was just as well.

She hadn't told her friends of her reluctance to get involved with a man, because that might lead to revelations about her troubled past. Eventually, she supposed it would come up, but better later than sooner. Much as she longed for complete acceptance by these women, she knew that relationships took time to grow. For now, she preferred to tread carefully.

A breeze carried the scent of salt air, and she spotted a couple of gulls wheeling overhead. As the path turned downhill toward the harbor, Jennifer slowed to avoid jostling the baby. Lori trotted ahead, stopped and began hopping up and down impatiently.

"What's gotten into you?" Samantha asked.

Instead of answering, Lori waved her left hand.

"Drying your nail polish?" Jennifer guessed.

A flash of light refracted from a diamond on Lori's finger. Sam halted in her tracks. "Oh, my gosh! She's wearing a ring!"

"Jared proposed last night. Doesn't he have fabulous taste?" Lori cried. "I mean the ring, not me. Although he's got good taste there, too, I guess!"

Jennifer wished this couple every happiness. Yet the thought of planning a future with a man she loved was almost too painful to contemplate.

Until last night, she'd believed her crushed dreams were safely locked away. Then Ian had filled her home with the deep rumble of his laugh and the challenging glint in his eyes. A reminder of what she'd dreamed of and lost.

With an effort, Jennifer broke through her memories. "That's great," she told Lori.

"Have you set a date?" asked Samantha, who'd already offered her congratulations.

"I've always dreamed of a Christmas wedding."

"That's only a few months off."

"We'll have a simple church ceremony," Lori assured them.

"What about the reception?" Sam inquired as they descended to the quay bordered by quaint shops. "How're you going to find a place on such short notice?"

Lori beamed. "Esther offered to host it at her house. She's my matron of honor. Have you seen their place? It's like something out of a magazine."

Jennifer had met Esther Franco, Tony's wife, a couple of times. A deputy district attorney, the woman exuded confidence, but much as Jennifer wanted to like her, she'd noticed that Esther always seemed to be gazing past the person she was talking to, as if seeking someone more interesting.

To be fair, they'd met at crowded social events. Perhaps Tony's wife *had* been expecting someone else.

"That was generous. Maybe she's not as self-centered as I took her for." As usual, Samantha didn't bother to soft-pedal her opinions. "And they do have a gorgeous house on the bluffs."

"She was the second person I called, after my mother. We've been best friends since high school," Lori said as they neared their favorite coffee shop.

"I'm glad to hear she's got a warm side," Samantha told the bride-to-be. "First I've seen of it, though."

"She *is* hard to talk to," Jennifer ventured.

Lori shrugged. "She's ambitious, and she can come across as abrasive. But she was *thrilled* that I asked her. Considering that they'll have a new baby in the house, I couldn't believe she offered to have the reception there."

A new baby, and not even pregnant. *At least Esther and I have that much in common,* Jennifer reflected ruefully. Although the staff tried not to gossip, there'd been a lot of curiosity when the news spread that the Francos had contracted with a surrogate to carry their child.

"She probably already has a nanny lined up," Samantha mused. "I hope two high-powered attorneys can manage to spend enough time with their kid so it recognizes their faces."

Jennifer smiled at her friend's exaggeration. "I bet they'll both melt the moment they see that baby. How could they help it?" As Lori held the coffee shop door, she eased the stroller over the threshold. "Oops-a-daisy," she cooed to Rosalie.

"Have a seat," Sam said. "I'll pick up your usual. My treat, since you're being such a good mom."

Jennifer thanked her and found a table with a view of the harbor. Along the wharf, boats bobbed at anchor, while farther out sails dotted the water. Sitting indoors, she missed the sounds and smells of the sea, but the fall air was a bit cool for the baby.

An older woman paused to beam at Rosalie. "Oh, how adorable!"

"Thank you." It seemed simplest not to bother with explanations.

The woman gazed down wistfully. "Brings back such sweet memories." With a sigh, she tore herself away.

A few minutes later, Samantha arrived with coffee and biscotti, followed by Lori with a cup of chai. Once again, Jennifer felt a wave of gratitude for her new friends. At her previous job as assistant PR director for a medical center, she'd occasionally gone to a movie or club with other women, but no one had clicked.

These two had accepted her at once. Their personalities seemed to blend, and they all enjoyed taking weekly walks that balanced exercise with self-indulgence.

Recalling her hesitant reaction to Lori's good news, Jennifer felt a twinge of guilt, even though she doubted the others had noticed. To show interest, she returned the discussion to the wedding plans. "Have you chosen your colors yet?"

"I want to get Esther's opinion first." From Lori's spiced milk tea, Jennifer caught a whiff of cinnamon and cloves. "I nearly forgot to ask! Would you two be my bridesmaids?"

"I'd love to," Samantha said.

"I'm honored." Jennifer meant that from the heart. "I've never been in a wedding."

"Seriously?" Lori asked. "I've been in four. Esther's, of course, and three of my sisters'. The other two aren't married yet."

Samantha rested her chin on her hand. "With five sisters, you'll have a lot of bridesmaids."

Lori shook her head. "Just you two and Esther. My sisters have been total snots the past few years. We have this love-hate thing, because I was always disciplining them, growing up."

"But family's important," Jennifer protested.

"Yeah, when they aren't being a pain in the butt." An uncharacteristic scowl darkened Lori's face. "I'm almost tempted not to invite them, but I'd never get away with that."

"You'd regret it if they didn't come," Sam advised. "Now, let's talk about happy stuff. Weddings ought to be pure bliss."

That remark from the usually hardheaded pediatrician surprised Jennifer. "I'm sure they should be fun, but isn't preparing for marriage the most important thing? Talking about your goals and making sure you're on the same page?"

"Jared and I don't need to do that," Lori told her. "We're perfect for each other."

"I can tell." Samantha nodded approval.

A quiver of doubt ran through Jennifer. Relationships always had issues, didn't they? "I realize you guys have a high level of compatibility, but…"

"Ooh, there's a romantic phrase! 'A high level of compatibility,'" Sam murmured.

"We have to compromise on *some* stuff," Lori agreed. "Like, we alternate picking movies. When it's his turn, I wear earplugs to block the explosions, and he teases me about my three-hankie tearjerkers. But on the big issues, no problem."

"Lucky you." Jennifer would consider herself incredibly fortunate to find a man she cared about who loved her in return. As for the issues, she'd be satisfied if they could meet each other halfway.

"I was a little worried when I told him I absolutely don't want kids," Lori conceded. "But he feels the same way."

"Really?" Jennifer dunked her biscotti into the coffee. It was messy but delicious.

"You know what medical school and residency are like. After putting in those long hours, he loves the freedom to just loll around on weekends with me."

"It's good you both know your own minds," the pediatrician said.

"We'll be best friends and lovers, forever."

Surely Lori and Jared ought to at least talk to a premarital counselor, Jennifer thought. On the other hand, perhaps her own mother's series of failed marriages had made her too cynical.

The chime of her cell phone sent her digging into her pocket. The name on the readout was Mark Rayburn. Hearing from the hospital director on a Saturday didn't bode well.

"Hello, Dr. Rayburn," she answered.

"Sorry for interrupting you on the weekend," he said. "How's the baby?"

Judging by the edge to his voice, he hadn't called simply to check on Rosalie, but Jennifer appreciated his concern. "She's fine. We're down at the harbor."

"We could really use you here." He released an exasperated breath. "That video's all over the Internet. We've had two more babies relinquished this morning."

"Really? Oh, my goodness."

"Social Services can't send anyone out yet and—excuse me?" He broke off, and she heard him talk to someone in the background. Then, into the phone: "Number three just arrived."

"Three safe haven babies in one day?" That was unheard of. "I'll get there as fast as I can."

"Tell him I'm coming, too," added Samantha, who'd obviously picked up the gist of the conversation.

Jennifer relayed that information over the phone.

"Good," Mark responded distractedly. "Mostly I'm worried about the press showing up."

"I'll do my best to keep a lid on things." They needed to get the babies settled into the nursery quickly. She doubted she'd be able to exercise much control if the wrong person got wind of this.

Such as Ian. Jennifer almost wished she hadn't encouraged him to stay and chat last night. What if he called her at the wrong moment and she let something slip? She'd have to be very, very careful.

By the time the administrator rang off, Samantha and Lori were clearing away the cups and napkins. "I'll take the baby for the day," Lori promised.

"But you don't like kids."

"Oh, they're cute when they're tiny." Her friend grinned. "They can't talk back yet."

"I wish I could say the same for reporters," Jennifer grumbled.

With her friends, she set off on the return hike. Pushing the stroller uphill got tougher at every step, which, Jennifer figured, was a pretty good indication of how this day was likely to go.

Chapter Five

Ian spent Saturday morning working on the celebrity divorce story. It involved a rock idol and his actress wife who were engaged in a vicious and very public child custody battle.

He had trouble imagining two things: a) that there was anything left to write about people whose every move was targeted by paparazzi, and b) that anybody cared. Okay, so the husband, known by the stage name of Riff, had a talent for playing guitar and singing, and the wife starred in big box office romantic comedies. That hardly qualified them as endlessly fascinating.

His brother-in-law disagreed. "You've got a talent for this sort of thing," Viktor DeJong said through Ian's hands-free phone as he drove south from L.A. toward an Anaheim hotel. Riff—real name: Rudolph Farnsworth—was scheduled to sign autographs at a children's charity event, and there were rumors that Mrs. Riff, aka Lacy Mirabeau, might show up.

"This is a waste of my time and everyone else's," Ian retorted. "What can possibly happen except that two people who once loved each other will hurl nasty accusations back and forth?"

"That's exactly what I'm hoping for," Viktor told him. "By the way, Anni says hi."

"Same to her."

"Great job on the baby story, by the way. Everyone's picking it up." His brother-in-law spoke flawless English, despite being a Belgian native. "Think you can drum up a new twist there over the weekend?"

"I'll try." Ian wouldn't mind seeing Jennifer again. Okay, if he were being honest, he'd very much like to see her.

At the hotel, he parked and slung the camera bag over his shoulder. Pierre was busy today chasing an Oscar-winning director and his new girlfriend, an actress barely on the right side of eighteen. Although Ian preferred to focus on reporting, he was capable of taking his own pictures.

Indoors, he wove through clumps of tourists towing children in Disneyland T-shirts. Near the ballroom, he glimpsed TV lights ahead and quickened his pace.

There stood Lacy Mirabeau, blond hair gleaming as she posed for an array of cameras. "It's typical of Riff to let down a children's charity," she was saying. "He hardly ever shows up for visitation with his own children." Beside her, a young man who must have been either her manager or publicist nodded at every word.

A woman wearing a press badge called out, "Didn't he call in sick with food poisoning? That's what his Web site says."

"Probably from eating his new girlfriend's cooking," Lacy sniped,

Ian activated his pocket digital recorder and got busy angling to catch the actress on camera. Being tall had advantages in a situation like this, he noted as he peered over his colleagues' heads.

The rest of the impromptu press conference proceeded pretty much by rote, from Ian's perspective. A few quotes and quite a lot of preening by the actress. On his smart phone, a scan of the musician's Web site revealed that, yes, he did claim to have food poisoning.

Ian uploaded his pictures to Flash News/Global, along with captions and an article hastily batted out on his netbook. He chalked the whole thing up as another mindless item to titillate a public that, in a bygone era, would have been well enough acquainted with their neighbors to gossip about *them* instead of celebrities.

Man, am I getting jaded, he mused as he returned to his car. He visualized baby Rosalie cradled in Jennifer's arms. What a breath of fresh air they were.

Political upheaval and wars and natural disasters weren't the only things that mattered. There were also the quiet, intimate moments that rarely qualified as news, moments that he'd glimpsed on the sidewalks and streets of cities around the world. A bride arriving at a church. Parents bringing a baby home from the hospital. Aging couples strolling hand in hand.

From jaded to sentimental. *That* had been a fast transition.

Well, Viktor had urged him to follow up the baby story. Easy enough, since Anaheim lay more than halfway between L.A. and Safe Harbor. But he had no intention of encroaching on Jennifer's privacy.

He recalled the angle he'd contemplated last night.

A giant corporation buys a community hospital and turns it into a moneymaking machine. That's got to rub somebody the wrong way. That somebody was the chief of pediatrics, unless he missed his guess.

Perhaps Dr. Forrest was on-site today. Worth a visit. If he didn't find her, he might luck into another staffer with a beef.

And if he happened to run into Jennifer, that would be even luckier. Because no matter how many arguments Ian mustered against seeing her again, his spirits leaped at the prospect.

ON THE FIFTH FLOOR, Jennifer and Samantha found Dr. Rayburn pacing the hall outside the administrative offices. His polo shirt and jeans testified to the fact that he'd rushed to the hospital on his day off.

"One of the moms is still in Tony Franco's office, signing paperwork," he informed them.

"Where are the babies?" Samantha asked.

"In the nursery. We'll keep them for the weekend. The corporation's not happy about providing unreimbursed services, but what else can we do?" The administrator didn't seem to expect a response. "Let's hope this whole thing blows over fast. Most hospitals don't receive more than one or two safe haven babies a month."

"That isn't the real problem," the pediatrician snapped. "It's these young women who didn't receive proper care in the first place. How many of them even saw a doctor or received any counseling during their pregnancies?"

"You can't hold me responsible for that!" Mark growled. "For heaven's sake, Sam, don't start on one of your social justice crusades."

"What better time?" she retorted.

Samantha had been grumbling about the hospital's official reopening for weeks, and Jennifer knew Mark felt pressure from higher-ups to keep everything running smoothly. Still, she'd never before seen them argue openly.

"The tension's getting to all of us," Jennifer said. "Let's focus on the problem at hand, okay?"

For a moment, her friend seemed on the verge of disagreeing. Then she shrugged. "You're right. I'll go take a look at those newborns."

"I'd appreciate it." Mark watched his fiery critic march down the hall. "I admire her principles, but we have to watch the bottom line. Too many hospitals are closing for lack of money. That doesn't serve the community, either."

Jennifer had no intention of taking sides. "Have you heard from the press?" she asked.

"The local paper inquired about you and Rosalie. I said you weren't giving interviews." Distractedly, the doctor reached up to loosen his tie and then apparently realized he wasn't wearing one. "As far as I can tell, nobody's gotten word of today's relinquishments, and I'd like to keep it that way."

"If it comes up, I think our response should be that almost all hospitals, fire departments and police stations accept these babies," Jennifer said. "There's nothing unusual here."

"Do you think you should put out a press release?"

"Let's not go looking for trouble," she advised.

"Good point."

Down the corridor, a door opened and Tony emerged

with a chubby young woman. As with Mark, his jeans and plaid shirt formed a stark contrast to his usual buttoned-down appearance.

"Thank you for signing the papers," he told his companion. "You have fourteen days to change your mind. If you decide you want to keep your baby, please call the number on my card."

"I can't. Sorry. Please find someone to love him." Head lowered, she hurried away.

Jennifer's chest ached. What circumstances had forced the girl into this? she wondered.

"What about the other two moms?" the administrator asked. "Have they completed the formalities?"

"Sure did. I gave them a few bucks to buy lunch at the cafeteria," the attorney said. "Funny thing. They're cousins. They'd been covering for each other with their relatives and, if you can believe it, delivered each other's babies less than a day apart."

That distressed Jennifer. "Why didn't they come here to deliver?" The hospital treated indigent patients without charge.

"Cultural issues, I guess," Tony said. "They were thinking of leaving the babies on someone's doorstep until they saw the story about you and Rosalie. Good work."

Publicity did have its merits. "That was fortunate."

"I hope you referred them to a clinic to get birth control so this doesn't happen again. Heck, I'd be glad to see them myself." Mark was still a practicing obstetrician in addition to his administrative duties.

"Gave them a whole packet of referrals." Tony didn't sound optimistic, though.

Based on her own experiences years ago, Jennifer,

too, doubted they'd seek counseling. Telling *anyone* about her situation had been the furthest thing from her mind. Besides, finding a low-cost or free counselor wasn't exactly easy these days.

Mark glanced at her. "Sorry for calling you in. It doesn't appear that we'll need your services after all."

"I'm glad you did. It's important to keep me in the loop." She much preferred staying abreast of developments to learning about them after the fact.

The attorney lingered in the hallway. "If you don't mind my asking, who's minding the baby?"

"Lori Ross. She was with me when I got the call," Jennifer said. "Why?"

He ducked his head. "You may have heard that Esther and I are going to be parents. It's hard to get my head around it, to tell you the truth. Since a nanny can't be around 24/7, I wondered how parents cope in emergencies."

He was just considering that *now?* Although Tony had always struck her as likable, clearly he hadn't taken his responsibilities as a father seriously enough. "You should arrange for backup, perhaps a friend or relative. Besides, once you fall in love with your child, you might not want a nanny around so much, anyway."

He blinked in surprise. "It's a boy. I pictured us playing ball, doing guy stuff like that when he's older. Hadn't thought much about the baby stage."

Had he assumed Esther would turn into a doting mom? It wasn't her place to lecture the attorney, however, so Jennifer excused herself and took the elevator downstairs.

In the lobby, a small family sat huddled silently on

a pair of couches, perhaps awaiting the results of a loved one's surgery. The only other occupants she saw were a couple talking earnestly at one side.

Her throat clamped as, from this three-quarters angle, she recognized the man as Ian. In a dark blue sweater over an open-collared shirt, he looked appealingly rumpled. As for the woman, wavy blond hair secured in a ponytail identified her immediately as Samantha.

Surely her friend had better judgment than to expose the hospital and those young mothers to the glare of publicity. But if they weren't discussing this morning's relinquishments, why was Ian listening so intently?

Jennifer struggled to maintain professional composure as she sauntered over. When Ian spotted her, the welcome curve of his mouth warmed her.

Don't be a fool. He didn't come here to see you.

"Good morning, Mr. Martin." She narrowed her eyes warningly at Samantha. For heaven's sake, the pediatrician ought to know how much was at stake. "Am I interrupting?"

"Dr. Forrest has been explaining about the local shortage of services for poor women." He didn't sound terribly keen on the subject. Good.

"The press always focuses on the sensational," Samantha complained. "The public ought to pay attention to things that matter."

"If they did that, I'd be out of a job." Ian grinned. "Actually, that's not true. I prefer gritty stories to—no offense, Jennifer—fluffy public relations."

"Fluffy? Like fertility treatments that create families?" She broke off. No sense in jumping on her bandwagon with Ian. "What brings you here today?"

"Snooping," he said flatly. "Speaking of which, where's Rosalie?"

"With a friend. An R.N.," she added, in case he planned to put the information into a story.

"Heard from her birth mother?"

"Not a word."

"Well, it's been interesting, ladies." He clicked off the digital recorder he'd set on a low table.

"Are you aware that this hospital closed its low-cost family clinic?" Clearly unwilling to let him go, Samantha returned doggedly to her theme. "The community used to depend on us, back when we were designated not-for-profit."

Jennifer felt obligated to provide the opposing viewpoint. "Unfortunately, for a lot of hospitals, not-for-profit too often translates as broke."

Then, beyond Ian, she spotted two girls emerging from the cafeteria. Loose dresses failed to hide figures still bloated from pregnancy.

These must be the cousins. If Ian got hold of that item, it was exactly the type of gossipy item to draw tons of attention—the wrong sort.

Samantha was frowning in the girls' direction. "Speaking of young women we should be helping, take those—"

Jennifer had to distract Ian fast. "You came for a follow-up, right?" she blurted.

He focused on her. "Sure."

She rushed on, ignoring Samantha's blink of annoyance. "How about spending the day observing Rosalie and me?" *That would get him out of the hospital, at least.*

He regarded her with a twist of friendly skepticism. "I thought you were concerned about your privacy."

She had to answer before Samantha got a word in edgewise. "I'm more concerned about Rosalie's birth mother and her future adoptive parents, whoever they may be." She rested a hand lightly on Samantha's shoulder. "It's their privacy we need to protect."

Her friend's taut muscles yielded. "That's true."

"I still don't get why you're willing to talk to me," Ian said.

"I'm offering you the story you came for. That's my job."

He studied her dubiously. "Or you're trying to distract me. I'd like to hear what Dr. Forrest was about to say."

"Dr. Forrest is finished talking." Samantha rose. "I tend to run at the mouth when I get on my soapbox."

Outside Ian's range of vision, the cousins paused at a gift kiosk to examine a display of teddy bears. Would they never leave?

"Of course, if you aren't interested in Rosalie, we're done here," Jennifer told him. "Nice seeing you again."

"Whoa." On his feet, he said, "So you simply decided to cooperate with me? Hard to buy, Jennifer."

"We've had a lot of reporters inquiring about Rosalie." Slight exaggeration. "One way or the other, we'll have to satisfy the public's curiosity, and it's safer for her to be around a single reporter. You're the lucky designee." Gripping her purse strap, she awaited Ian's response.

He cocked an eyebrow. "I can stick around all day? Take pictures?"

"Within reason. I don't want my every comment splashed across the Web."

"I'll be discreet."

Their gazes locked. In Ian's half-joking expression, she saw both appeal and danger. But at least she'd achieved her goal—the young mothers were disappearing through the front exit.

"When do we start?" he asked.

Before she could answer, she noticed Tony and Mark across the room. "We start with me getting my boss's approval."

"I'll wait here."

"Great." Jennifer went to explain the situation. She was careful to avoid laying any blame on Samantha.

"You're sure you're okay having that man hanging around your place?" the administrator asked.

"We don't want to put you in any uncomfortable circumstances, being alone with this guy," Tony added.

"He seems pleasant enough. We had a nice chat after the opening." No reason to mention that it had involved a late-night drink at her kitchen table.

Mark gave his consent and wished her a good weekend. As the men departed, Jennifer braced herself. She'd been so intent on running damage control that she hadn't fully considered what lay ahead—a whole afternoon of keeping up her guard

Exactly how discreet could she expect Ian to be? Jennifer had no illusions about how easily a misstep might be magnified in print or in a photo.

Her phone rang. Please, not more reporters, she thought, and then she saw the display. "Lori? I'm nearly done here," she answered as she crossed the lobby.

"It's the baby," her friend said breathlessly. "She's

fussy and she feels hot. I'm afraid she's coming down with something."

Everything else vanished from Jennifer's mind. "Let me grab Samantha." Praying that the problem wasn't serious, she hurried to explain and hand over her phone.

The pediatrician asked Lori a few questions. "We'll be right there," she concluded. To Jennifer and Ian, she said, "It doesn't sound serious, but any elevated temperature in a newborn should be checked."

Jennifer folded away the phone. "Let's get moving."

"Shall I follow in my car?" Ian asked.

Oh, heavens, she'd given him permission to tag along without considering that something might go amiss. Too late to back out now.

"Whatever," Jennifer replied. "Let's *go*."

"You're really worried."

"Of course! She's my..." She'd almost said "daughter." "My responsibility. Now, let's hurry," she concluded, and led the others on a dash to the parking structure.

Suddenly, spending a day under Ian's scrutiny didn't seem important at all. The only thing that mattered was the baby.

Chapter Six

Ian knew when a source was holding out on him. Jennifer had offered herself as a subject because she feared the pediatrician might spill something sensitive. Of course, it might be nothing more than a few uncharitable remarks about the administration, but he'd like to be sure.

Pleased as he was at the chance to follow up on the baby story, he still meant to keep his eyes open this weekend. His promise to be discreet applied to embarrassing personal stuff, not to revelations regarding the hospital.

In all honesty, though, his interest wasn't entirely professional. When he'd glimpsed Jennifer in the lobby, the lilt of her movements had made him forget, just for a second, why he was there.

Spending the day with her would be a pleasure. And he hoped she might enjoy his company, too.

In his rented car, Ian followed Jennifer's sedan to an apartment building half a block past her condo. Cozy, the way these women lived practically on top of one another.

Ian recalled reading somewhere that cities were a series of interlocking small towns consisting of neighborhoods, extended families, friendship groups and coworkers. Sounded reasonable, although outside his personal experience. Aside from a few friends scattered around the globe, his only meaningful connections were with Anni and Viktor and with his parents. They'd retired to the Indian city of Amritsar, which they'd fallen in love with while visiting the Golden Temple.

Like them, Ian adapted easily to new locales. Yet as he trailed Jennifer and Samantha up an exterior staircase, he felt as if he were about to be admitted to a *truly* exotic realm: the private world of a group of women.

The door opened on a rumpled apartment. A blanket lay spread on the couch, where pillows hedged in the baby. On the floor, clean, folded laundry filled a basket, while the floral scents of household products perfumed the air.

An irritable cry arose from the sofa. Restless motions threatened to kick aside the baby's coverings.

"She's still hot and you can see that she's restless," said the woman who'd ushered them in. He recognized her red-brown hair, freckles and no-nonsense expression from the previous night.

"I'll take a look." Carrying a medical kit, Samantha Forrest headed for her little patient.

The nurse surveyed Ian disapprovingly. "What's *he* doing here?"

"Lori, this is Ian," Jennifer said in a chiding tone. "Before you called, I invited him to do a story." Then, as if unable to contain her anxiety, she hurried to the couch, leaving the two of them alone in the doorway.

"Sorry." Lori's expression didn't strike Ian as particularly regretful, however. "Nothing personal."

"I understand." He swung his attention to the couch, where Samantha had removed the pillows blocking his view of Rosalie.

"Good heavens, she's wrapped up like a mummy," the doctor said.

"It was cold this morning," Lori explained.

"Brisk, I suppose. But it's comfortable in here." As the pediatrician began unbundling the baby, Ian took out his camera.

Lori scowled. "Put that *away.*"

He hesitated.

Hovering fretfully at the doctor's elbow, Jennifer weighed in. "Hardly appropriate, Ian. What if she's truly sick?"

"You're right." He put the camera back in its case.

While he'd conducted plenty of touchy interviews, Ian had never been in a situation where he felt quite like this. Experience had programmed him to treat every occurrence as a story angle and every image as a photo opportunity. Instead, he ached to soothe away the worry on Jennifer's face. To forget about reporting and become part of the events instead of observing them.

He couldn't allow that. Not only would it be unprofessional, but at some level it might prove Viktor right about Ian's true calling. Damn it, he wasn't some mushy human-interest writer.

"Let's find out what her temperature's doing." Samantha rolled the baby onto her tummy. Whoa! She was going to stick the thermometer *where?*

"Can't you take a reading from her ear?" At Ian's last checkup, that was what the nurse had done. And a good thing, too.

"It might not be accurate in a baby this young," the doctor said. "Their ear canals can be rather wet."

"Her temp was over 100," Lori advised. "I took it under the armpit."

"This will be more accurate." Samantha inserted the thermometer.

The baby squawked. "You're hurting her!" Jennifer protested.

"Calm down, Mommy. She's fine."

"What's a normal temperature for a newborn?" Ian asked.

"Under the armpit, which is a cooler part of the body, normal would be 97.5 to 99.5. This way, anything under 100.2 is normal." When the thermometer beeped, Samantha withdrew it. "Right at 100. She's fine."

"I don't understand," Lori said. "A few minutes ago, her temp was high and she felt hot."

"Infants can get feverish if they're overly bundled." After washing her hands, the doctor peered into the baby's throat, ears and nose. "I don't see any sign of infection."

The little creature had calmed. "She seems a lot happier," Ian observed. "I guess I would be, too, if you took that thing out of my...never mind."

Jennifer burst into a free, shimmering laugh. "Ian!"

"Relieved that she's okay?" he asked.

She pressed a hand to her heart. "It was worse than being sick myself. She's so helpless."

Could she have bonded with the little one in such a short period? Ian didn't see how. *But it will make a great story.*

Samantha covered the baby lightly. "Not that I'm criticizing, Lori, but I think she was simply uncomfortable. As a nurse, you should know that."

"I work with moms, not babies," Lori grumbled.

"You took care of your little sisters."

"Not until they were cranky toddlers. Mom hogged the cute newborns for herself."

"No wonder you don't want kids," Samantha observed wryly.

"None of this belongs in your article," Jennifer told Ian. He held up his hands in surrender. "I promise."

"Want to hold her now?" Samantha asked.

"Oh, yes! Please." Jennifer reached out eagerly. This time when Ian took out his camera no one objected.

As Jennifer gathered the infant close, Rosalie gazed upward with what Ian, through the lens, could have sworn was devotion. What a great shot. As for the tug inside his chest, well, he'd never claimed to be *entirely* without emotions.

"Keep a close watch on her for the next twenty-four hours. Of course, I'm sure you planned to do that, anyway," Samantha said. "Call me if you have any concerns."

"I'd be happy to help you," Lori added. "Even though I screwed up, I really am good with kids."

"Oh, I have in-house help today." Jennifer regarded Ian mischievously. "You're game for changing diapers, right?"

He captured her expression on camera, less for the Internet than because he found her so engaging. "I'm a fast learner." Still, he hoped she was joking.

"Oh! I nearly forgot. Is everybody up for shopping this afternoon at Brides and Maids?" Lori asked. "You don't have to spend every minute with this reporter— excuse me, with Ian—do you, Jennifer?"

The PR director gave her friend an apologetic shrug. "Not today. I did promise."

"Today's the only day Esther's available, and she *is* the matron of honor."

"Any reason I can't tag along?" Ian asked.

"You're kidding, right? A guy in a bridal shop?" Lori's face scrunched. "Everybody'll think you're the groom. Oh, what the hell. But you can't write about it."

"No problem."

After agreeing on a time, the little group dispersed. Ian photographed Jennifer strapping the baby into her car seat, even for a mere half-block drive.

Ian wondered if she was really thinking about keeping the baby. If so, the public would love it.

Entering Jennifer's condo a few minutes later, he noticed details that had escaped him before. A vase of silk flowers on an end table. An arched mirror on one wall, surrounded by small framed prints. He didn't see any family photographs, though.

"I'll be happy to e-mail you my best shots," he said as she sank onto the couch, cuddling the baby.

"That would be wonderful." Slowly, she added, "I'll pass them along to her adoptive parents. I'm sure they'll appreciate my documenting this part of her life."

She sounded sad. Or perhaps simply tired. "You should catch a nap."

She straightened, visibly shaking off her torpor. "Not yet. This little pumpkin needs a bath."

Ian pretended to sniff the air. "Hey, I've gone for weeks more fragrant than that."

"Well, we aren't in the trenches. Besides, after being overheated, it'll make her feel better." She didn't explain how she knew that, but he supposed it made sense. "The linen closet's right over there. Bring a bath towel, a hand towel and a washcloth, would you?"

He tucked away his camera and obeyed. Incredibly neat linen closet, he mused when he examined it, with the towels perfectly folded and stacked. Hard as he tried not to disturb anything, he left the contents slightly mussed.

Arms laden with towels, he whistled his way into the kitchen.

"Made a mess, didn't you?" Jennifer commented from the counter, where she was setting out baby products.

"Sorry?"

"Whistling. A sure sign of guilt." She jerked her head toward an open spot. "Set those here, will you?"

He chuckled. "You must have brothers."

"A half brother. Eight years younger. A wild child till he joined the army. I have no idea how he survived basic training." She spread out the bath towel.

"Where's the tub?" Ian could swear he'd brought in a baby-size bathtub last night. It would fit perfectly into the sink, right below the window.

"She's too little to sit up yet. I have to sponge-bathe her." With great care, Jennifer lifted Rosalie from the baby carrier.

Surely women weren't born with all this knowledge. "How did you know she was too little for the bathtub?"

"I looked it up on the hospital's Web site." She removed the infant's sleeper and tossed it aside. "We've got a whole section devoted to baby care."

"And here I had you figured for a mythical earth mother."

"I'm far from that."

Remembering why he was here, Ian retrieved the camera. As he focused on the pair, he noticed how a filtered pool of sunlight enveloped them, giving Jennifer's olive skin the sheen of an old master painting.

"You're impressive," he told her as he framed shot after shot.

"She's such a sweetheart. I could swear she's shifting to make it easier for me to wash her." Jennifer's eyes never left the baby. "They have personalities from the moment they're born. Maybe even sooner."

Her voice caught. Startled, Ian lowered the camera. "Is something wrong?"

"Not at all." Yet there it was again, that trace of melancholy. Because she had to give up Rosalie?

"You're thinking of keeping her?" Ian ventured.

"It's what her birth mother wanted," she conceded. "Although that isn't realistic."

"True. I mean, this whole thing just fell in your lap," he mused. "It's not as if you were desperate for a child."

"How do you know what I'm desperate for?"

The sharpness in her voice startled him. Apparently, he'd hit a nerve. "I guess I don't know."

Tossing the washcloth in the sink, she began drying Rosalie. Gradually, she relaxed enough to murmur nonsense syllables to the baby.

"Is that some kind of code?" Ian asked, hoping to restore their easy banter. "My sister used to speak that way to my nieces, until they got big enough to talk back."

"How old are they?"

"Six and eight." Guiltily, he recalled that he'd missed their birthdays this past year. They'd popped up on his digital calendar, but he'd never gotten around to buying presents. Well, he'd make up for it at Christmas, if he wasn't in Asia or Africa.

The prospect of being dispatched to a war zone failed to stir the usual excitement. He'd really like to spend Christmas with family for a change.

"You've been standing there staring into space for quite a while." Jennifer lifted a fully clad Rosalie from the counter. Either she worked fast or he really had dimmed out. "Memories? Or just bored?"

"Not bored." She seemed to expect more, so he added, "It hit me that my sister's kids are growing up fast. As for Anni, I can't believe she'll be thirty-five next month."

"Since she's your twin, that means you'll be thirty-five, too," she pointed out. "Traumatic?"

"Feeling my mortality," he conceded.

"Bullets didn't do that?"

"Oddly, no. Surviving a close call merely reinforced my sense of being lucky." Ian collected the dirty linens from the counter and set them atop the washing machine in the corner.

Jennifer yawned.

"I'm glad you find my getting shot so tedious," he said.

She favored him with a sleepy smile. "I think I'll take that nap now." Her expression sobered. "Darn. I can't go to sleep yet."

"Why not?"

"I have to make sure Rosalie doesn't spike a fever. They can come and go in babies," she explained.

The doctor *had* suggested keeping a close watch. "I can set up my netbook in the living room. If she fusses, I'll wake you."

Standing in the center of the kitchen, she rocked from one foot to the other. "At this age, she might not make much noise even if she gets sick."

"I'll set my watch for every half hour and feel her forehead. How's that?"

After a tick of hesitation, Jennifer nodded. "Thanks. If you get hungry, there are nutrition drinks in the fridge."

Nutrition drinks? "I never heard beer referred to that way before."

Her nose wrinkled. "No beer. Just diet supplements. And some leftovers from last night."

That sounded better. "I'll be fine. Go rest."

In the living room, she tucked the baby into the bassinet. "If she doesn't get sick, she'll probably sleep for an hour or so. When she wakes, come upstairs and get me."

"Sure. Go!" If he didn't issue orders, Ian suspected she'd hang around until she collapsed.

"Here's Samantha's phone number." She scribbled it on a pad. "If there's a serious problem…"

Folding his arms, he feigned a glare. "Did anyone ever mention that you're overresponsible?"

Apologetically, Jennifer laid a hand on his forearm. A current quivered through Ian. "I don't mean to impose. It isn't your job to babysit."

"It's not yours, either, but you're acting like a real mother," Ian said. She stood so close, he could have brushed a kiss across her mouth. "You can trust me with her. Go get some rest."

She moved away. "Call me the instant she wakes."

"Count on it."

After Jennifer went upstairs, Ian checked on Rosalie for good measure. She was slumbering blissfully.

He set his watch timer and opened his computer on the coffee table. While uploading pictures from the camera, he listened to the hum of a car passing on the street and the rise and fall of voices from passersby. How strange and wonderful to be writing about Jennifer and the baby for a world of readers who understood, as he was only beginning to, that beneath the tranquil surface of an ordinary California town stirred the same dreams and longings that gave meaning to people's lives everywhere.

Quite a human-interest story. Viktor was going to love it.

Chapter Seven

When Jennifer awoke, bright afternoon sunlight peeped through the cracks in the blinds, and the bedside clock display showed she'd slept for an hour and a half. She sat up with the anxious sense of having missed a key appointment.

The baby. How could she have left her little boy so long? Where was Edward?

Not Edward. Rosalie. Not her little boy, but Sunny's baby girl.

It had been a long while since she'd dreamed about the baby she'd lost. She wasn't even certain that she *had* dreamed about him, but tending to Rosalie had aroused that old anguish.

Well, she'd better go check. No telling whether Ian had kept his promise to check every half hour, or simply figured it was enough if he didn't burn down the house.

Impatiently, Jennifer paid a quick trip to the bathroom. By the time she finished brushing her hair and restoring her smudged makeup, the silence from downstairs had begun to worry her. She'd heard of a father who'd driven to work, forgotten about day care and left his child strapped in the car's rear seat. What if Ian had left Rosalie alone?

She flew to the open staircase. Below, she glimpsed a strong figure seated on the sofa. But the bassinet— empty. Where was the baby?

"Ian!" At the bottom, seeing the warning finger pressed to his lips, she halted.

Then she noticed the blue bulge of the cloth baby holder strapped across his chest. A cherubic creature rested blissfully against him, her eyes closed, lulled by the gentle swell of his breathing.

"You should have called me," Jennifer murmured, more from a sense of obligation than because she wanted to disturb this cozy scene.

"I tried. You were sound asleep. Nice outfit, by the way." Ian's amused glance made her keenly aware of the silky tank top clinging to her body. She'd forgotten to put on the coordinated sweater, she realized.

At the rumble of his voice, Rosalie stirred, but snuggled down again with a happy sigh. Ian's long legs twitched as if he longed to stretch them. He didn't, though.

How sweet would it be if this child belonged to her, and a deep love united her with this man? whispered a traitorous voice inside Jennifer. Ian was exactly her type, from his lean, rangy body to the ironic tilt of his head. Not to mention the tantalizing hint of the rogue about him.

Exactly her type, all right. The type that always let her down, or, worse, *led* her down the wrong path.

She dragged herself out of her reflections. "How's the follow-up story coming?"

"Just e-mailed it, as a matter of fact." Good thing

she'd given him her Wi-Fi pass code. Or maybe not, depending on what he'd written.

"Am I going to hate myself or you in the morning?" Jennifer asked.

"You'll love it. All sweetness and light." He surveyed her with a sparkle of sympathy. "How're you feeling?"

"Better," she admitted.

Cautiously, he stood and unstrapped the baby holder. "Can I set her in the bassinet in this?"

"I'll take her." Jennifer couldn't wait to hold the little one.

As he shifted Rosalie into her grasp, Jennifer felt his body heat form a protective circle around the three of them. Her head swam from the combined effect of his aftershave and the baby's powdery scent.

"You sure you're okay?" Ian asked.

"Naps leave me groggy." Taking regular breaths to dissipate the wooziness, she busied herself adjusting the cloth straps.

"I'll do that." He reached around her, strong hands fiddling with the Velcro. Jennifer fought the urge to rest her cheek on his chest, as Rosalie had done moments earlier. "All set?"

She straightened and felt the tug of well-balanced weight. "Just right."

Ian moved away. "I'm afraid I have to leave on business. I'm sure your friends will miss me at the bridal shop, but we'll just have to disappoint them."

"Business? It's Saturday," Jennifer protested. But she was being foolish. "I mean, of course. Now that you've written your story."

He wedged the computer inside a leather bag. "I'd

be happy to come back and help you with the baby tonight. To make sure she's okay. I'll be completely off duty, I promise."

"It won't be much fun, I'm afraid." But she wanted him to stay over, more than she ought to.

"Let me worry about that." He picked up the bag. "I've got an interview and then another story to write. I'm not sure what time I'll get here. Could be seven or eight."

"That works for me. I'll probably be out with my friends till dinnertime, anyway," Jennifer said.

With a wave, he strode out. He moved gracefully, and she noticed his enticingly slim butt. What was wrong with her? Jennifer wondered. Why so susceptible to an obviously unsuitable man?

Yet as she hummed to soothe Rosalie, she had to admit he'd proved to be much more than the pretty-boy reporter she'd initially taken him for. But who was he deep inside?

Temporary, that was what, Jennifer answered her own question. And she didn't intend to forget it.

ELEANOR WYCLIFF, EX-WIFE of corrupt federal judge Brandon Wycliff, occupied a Beverly Hills home that could double as a hotel. On their way inside, Ian and Pierre had to pass muster with a housekeeper, a security guard and Mrs. Wycliff's personal attorney.

"I'm so mad I could spit," the patrician woman announced when they entered the vast living room. She stood posed by a giant fireplace, silvering hair upswept, designer pantsuit flowing.

"For the sake of their children, my client has kept silent about her husband's legal problems," noted the attorney, a compactly built man with the dark tan of a tennis aficionado. Or possibly a golfer.

"What's changed?" Ian activated his digital recorder.

Eleanor smacked her palm on the mantel, nearly dislodging what appeared to be a very expensive glass sculpture. "Our seventeen-year-old daughter, Libby, is an aspiring actress. I just learned that one of Brandon's unsavory associates tried to persuade her to act in a dirty movie. My ex had no business even introducing her to such a man!"

Unsavory associates. Porno films. A judge, already under indictment for taking bribes, who failed to protect his teenage daughter. Quite a tale.

Ian got comfortable on a sofa bigger than the queen-size bed in his motel room. He spent the next two hours, between shrimp and lobster snacks, excellent coffee and Godiva chocolates produced by the housekeeper, probing the scandalous misconduct of the one-time judge.

Not only had the man accepted bribes from gangland figures, Mrs. Wycliff declared, he'd spent weekends in Palm Springs and Las Vegas with a crime boss and a handful of call girls. At home, his pockets had produced a damning series of casino receipts, telephone numbers scrawled in pink ink on scented scraps of paper, and small bags of white powder. She'd also found ladies' lingerie, handcuffs and assorted other paraphernalia among his things.

"Finally, I divorced him, but I kept quiet for our daughter's sake," she said. And to ensure a large divorce settlement, Ian suspected.

"Since discovering her daughter was endangered,

my client has turned over evidence to the U.S. Attorney's office," added her lawyer.

"What kind of evidence, exactly?" Ian asked.

Mrs. Wycliff waved a manicured hand. "I copied photographs I found on his computer. Of my husband in, shall we say, compromising positions. Would you like to see a few?"

They would indeed.

"Gives new meaning to the word *excess*," Pierre observed later as they emerged into the curving, palm-shaded driveway.

"Also the word *arrogance*." Ian never ceased to be amazed at the egotism of powerful figures who assumed they were above detection. "How could he do that to his family?"

Just before departing, they'd run into the daughter in the hall. A pretty teenager with spice-brown hair and wide-set gray eyes, she'd given them a startled, almost frightened stare. After briefly acknowledging their introductions, she'd fled to private quarters.

"Sure is a nice place." Pierre's gesture took in the sprawling Spanish-style home and the luxurious spill of greenery in one of the choicest locations in L.A.

"He didn't manage to keep it," Ian pointed out.

"I hear he bought another house just as fancy." Pierre sniffed. "When do you plan to file your story?"

"In a few hours." With so many issues at stake, not to mention the potential for libel, this called for more care than a quick account of a press conference.

"Fair enough. I'll be uploading the video pretty quick, but the editing will take a while. Coming to the office?"

"I'd rather work at my motel." On a prior visit to L.A,

Ian had tried writing in the cramped Flash News/Global quarters, but after being repeatedly stumbled into and interrupted, he'd decided he was better off in his room.

A short while later, he drove beneath the Rooms to Let—Weekly/Monthly sign as he pulled into the parking lot. He'd picked the location for its proximity to work, restaurants and freeways. The smell of exhaust hadn't bothered him, nor had the traffic noise.

Now he couldn't help picturing Jennifer's peaceful neighborhood. Planters spilling over with flowers. The scent of a sea breeze. A fridge full of food.

He could hardly wait to go back.

Inside, the room looked pretty much like every other cheap hotel or motel room around the globe. Thin mattress, stiff chair at a tiny table, small bathroom stocked with a few appliances, and a narrow closet displaying a few garments. A musty odor, overlaid with lemon cleanser, did nothing to improve the ambience.

Ian took out the computer. An hour later, he went out to the vending machines for peanut butter crackers, returned and resumed his task.

After finally hitting Send, he checked his watch. Nearly 8:00 p.m. Adding eleven hours made it 7:00 a.m. Sunday, Brussels time. Headquarters was staffed 24/7, so he placed a call via Internet phone to tell the editor to watch for the piece. Otherwise, it might sit in a queue until Monday.

To his surprise, Viktor's image appeared on the screen: broad cheekbones, sandy hair, a few wrinkles fanning from gray eyes. Ian switched on his Web cam and explained that he'd just sent the Judge Wycliff exclusive. "What brings you in on a Sunday?" he added.

"We're shuffling staff and I had to fill in." As managing editor, Viktor often served double duty. "The weekend news editor got transferred to Beijing, and his replacement had some personal business to finish up before relocating from Paris."

"Anni must be thrilled to have even less time with you," Ian joked.

"She understands. And is grateful to be out of this madhouse."

Was she really? Ten years ago, his sister had been as ambitious as Ian. Even after her marriage, she'd spent months working on a separate continent from her husband. Finally she'd reached the agonizing decision to quit in order to start a family. He'd always assumed she planned to start reporting again once the kids got older.

Viktor went on talking. "We moved your follow-up on baby Rosalie. It's already getting a great response from subscribers. There's something about an abandoned baby that hits people right in the gut."

"I'm sure it's a relief from reading about economic woes and bombings."

"You have to keep this story alive." The editor leaned back in his desk chair, nearly bumping the wall behind him.

Ian had promised to be off duty tonight. Still, he could pursue the story next week. "She plans to turn the baby over to Social Services on Monday."

"Don't wait for that. Get in touch with the birth mother. What's her name, Sunny? Find out her story. Who the father is. Why she dropped off the baby. Why she was so insistent on Jennifer becoming the mother."

Even as his instincts acknowledged Viktor's news

judgment, Ian's spirit rebelled. "In return for today's access, I promised Jennifer I'd respect her privacy."

"And so you will. But contacting the birth mother is another matter."

Ian doubted Jennifer would see it that way. "I think we've milked this enough. Why upset people's lives to write fluff?"

"Because it's fluff that people love to read about," his editor pressed. "By the way, did you know Armand Ephron is retiring?"

That caught Ian's attention. Armand, whose sun-creased and battered countenance was instantly recognizable worldwide, held the enviable position of writing his own column, "From the Fire." He had the freedom to choose stories anywhere on earth, from onetime interviews to in-depth investigations.

"Who's replacing him?" Ian asked.

On the screen, Viktor's jaw worked. "We're considering several possibilities."

Ian nearly stopped breathing at the implication. "Am I one of them?"

"I wouldn't have mentioned this if you weren't," his brother-in-law said.

Ian would kill for that position. Or at least maim someone. "What can I do to make my case?"

"The decision will be based on a body of work, not any one story," Viktor replied. "We're looking at a range of qualifications. Writing style. News instinct. The gift of stirring Internet buzz."

Suddenly, the ability to ferret out human-interest stories had become more than window dressing, Ian saw. He'd always considered Armand basically a hard-news guy, but now that he thought about it, the guy had a talent for finding the personal angle in the stories he reported.

"And you want me to track down this birth mother." Ian sighed.

"It isn't a test," the editor countered. "I'm just alerting you to put your best foot forward with all your stories this week. Bill and Mack have the final say."

They were Flash News/Global's executive editor and publisher, who'd jointly founded and obtained financing for the news service. No doubt Viktor would be asked for input, but he couldn't show favoritism.

The opportunity to land such a position might not recur for decades. "Thanks for the alert."

"You're welcome. Now, I'd better get to work on your latest opus."

Ian signed off, his thoughts in turmoil. While he didn't believe his entire future hung on this one story, he ran the risk of missing a bet if he backed off. Especially if the rest of the week proved slow in L.A. while some competitor in another locale hit the news jackpot.

Well, no use worrying. With luck, by tomorrow he'd figure out how to handle this situation. And luck generally came down on Ian's side.

Chapter Eight

"If Esther doesn't get here soon, I'll have to leave." Samantha fingered a sophisticated plum gown that stood out among the mostly pastel bridesmaids' dresses. "I'm giving a talk to a group of teenagers tonight and I need to review my notes."

Jennifer, who'd arrived five minutes late after misjudging how long it would take to get Rosalie ready, didn't feel qualified to criticize. Still, the matron of honor *was* twenty minutes overdue, especially annoying since they'd arranged this outing to suit her schedule.

Also, in the crowded shop, other customers had to keep sidling past the baby carriage. On the plus side, Rosalie seemed entranced by all the colors and movement.

Jennifer tried to picture Ian crammed in here with all these women, dresses, hats, stockings, veils and dye-to-match shoes. He'd probably be grinning his head off.

Holding a strapless white gown in front of her, Lori studied it in a full-length mirror. "She's flying to Washington tomorrow for a conference. I guess she got busy packing."

The saleslady who'd been trying to help them since they arrived regarded them with strained patience. "If you'd like to start trying on dresses, I'd be happy to put them in a changing room for you."

"Thanks, but not yet."

"Just let me know when you're ready." She moved off.

"I don't know if I want to go with traditional white." Lori frowned. "Esther's pushing for a theme of black-and-white. That seems a little severe to me."

"Whose wedding is this, anyway?" Samantha burst out. "Seriously, Lori! You're not nearly this nice to anyone else. Don't take that the wrong way. But you cut Esther an incredible amount of slack."

"She's been my best friend forever. And *her* wedding was fabulous, so I know she's got great taste." Lori sighed. "The thing is, after helping three of my sisters plan theirs, I'm sick of the usual color schemes."

"Which are your favorites?" Jennifer asked.

"Pink and purple, but Louise used those and Lana picked lavender and rose. I *can't* have a wedding like theirs." Her sisters' names all started with the letter *L*, Jennifer gathered. "I thought about a strictly Christmas theme, but red and green just doesn't work for me."

"These are smashing." Samantha indicated a set of gowns in silver for the bride and blue with silver trim for her attendants. "And they do fit the season."

"They're gorgeous. But if we decide on something, Esther will sweep in here and make us start over," moaned the bride-to-be.

"Oh, honestly!" Samantha scowled at a new arrival who bore a resemblance to Esther but, on closer inspection, proved to be a stranger. "No offense, but your best bud reminds me of a prom queen who thinks the whole world revolves around her."

Lori bristled. "Maybe it does."

"She is very accomplished," Jennifer said to ease the tension. "Doesn't she have a law degree from Stanford?"

"USC," Lori corrected.

"I've seen in the paper that she's prosecuting high-profile cases, so the district attorney's office obviously thinks well of her."

"You don't have to take her side," Samantha said. "You do PR for the hospital, not for the administrators' spouses."

Jennifer supposed she *had* been acting out of instinct. "I like Tony. I'm assuming he chose his wife wisely."

Lori's cell phone played a wedding march. She checked the display and demanded, "Where are you?"

"Ah, the queen deigns to address her subjects," Samantha muttered.

From Lori, there ensued a series of "ohs" and "yes, buts," concluding with, "You sure you can't stand plum? Well, I'm not sure I *care* that it'll clash with your Chinese red living room! Okay, fine."

"Unbelievable," Samantha said as their friend clicked off. "She wants the bridal party to match her decor?"

"We don't have to match," Lori explained. "Just not clash. She said silver and blue would be fine."

Samantha crossed her arms. "Esther's not coming?"

"She has to finish some last-minute paperwork before her trip." Lori appeared to be searching in vain for more justification. "I admit it's annoying…."

"Last-minute work she didn't know about when you talked to her an hour ago?" Samantha growled. She obviously didn't expect a reply, nor did she receive one.

The women tried on the silver-and-blue dresses, which, to Jennifer's eye, looked fantastic. Lori couldn't believe they'd hit the jackpot on their first shopping trip, but had to admit the bridal gown—one of three designs in silver—was everything she'd hoped for.

As Jennifer was changing into her street clothes, Rosalie let out a tiny cry. "Oh, dear. I fed her before we came. I can't believe she's hungry again already."

"You know what?" Lori said. "I'll have the shop put a two-week hold on these dresses. That way Esther can try hers on when she gets back from her trip."

"Good idea. Even Esther ought to be able to make her way in here by then," Samantha said.

"She's not like she seems. Honestly."

Samantha laid an arm around her friend's shoulders. "Don't let me dampen your spirits. This whole process should be a pleasure."

"She can be lots of fun when she's not so rushed," the bride-to-be added weakly.

"I'm sure she can. On rare occasions, possibly coinciding with odd phases of the moon, but let's not argue," Sam responded.

The three of them laughed. "Okay, she let me down," Lori conceded. "I don't know what's gotten into her."

"Maybe she's caught up in getting ready for the baby," Jennifer suggested.

The other women nodded. To Jennifer's relief, they parted on that conciliatory note.

Despite her affection for her new friends, it felt good to get home with Rosalie. Shopping with a baby along meant dividing her attention, and she yearned to enjoy the little one fully in the short time they had together.

Jennifer's throat tightened as, seated on the couch, she supported the baby in the crook of her arm and tilted the bottle. She dreaded the prospect of handing Rosalie over to a social worker. Already the little one had better control of her head and neck muscles, and a stronger sucking ability. Who would be holding her a week from now, or a month? Who would watch her take her first steps?

Tears filled Jennifer's eyes. Yet it was crazy to dwell on this. She had far too much else to think about.

After Rosalie finished nursing, she set the portable bassinet in her downstairs office and logged on to look for Ian's story on the Internet. To her surprise, a close-up photo of her with the baby dominated Flash News/ Global's home page. In the picture, delight animated Jennifer's expression, while the baby gazed back intently. Good heavens, why were they featured so prominently?

Ian began his story with Lori's anxious phone call and Jennifer's rush to the baby's side. A reader would get the impression she'd driven like a madwoman, obsessed with reaching the infant.

Dear heaven, how many people were reading this, and what would they think?

The rest of the story flowed smoothly, with more sweetness than she'd expected. Another photo high-lighted the sponge bath, while the text recapped Sunny's relinquishment on Friday. It also mentioned the hospital as a safe haven for mothers and babies.

Did Ian have to use those words again? Safe Harbor was no more a safe haven facility than any other hospital.

The public relations side of Jennifer's brain took over. How great an impact was this story having? She began to search the Web.

The account had been picked up by dozens of Web sites and blogs. Fortunately, the comments were generally positive. Most people seemed to find it the feelgood item of the moment.

Jennifer wished she felt equally good about the situation, but she didn't. Her discomfort had little to do with the relinquishment issue and everything to do with her past.

Since entering public relations, she'd understood that her name and face would occasionally appear in the media. So far, there'd been no repercussions. But the events of twelve years ago had left scars, not only in Jennifer's life, but on other people, too. People who might blame her for being involved with Frank when he ran afoul of the law. People who'd been injured and who might believe she'd gotten off too easily.

Frank remained in prison, where he belonged. Although she'd testified against him, she wasn't worried about him attempting to get retribution from behind bars or in the future. He'd seemed genuinely contrite for the harm he'd caused. But she didn't expect his other victims to forgive him—or her.

What if the press found out? That would cast a very different light on this warm, fuzzy story.

She ought to feel relief that, on Monday, she would hand over the baby to someone else, ending her involvement. Yet when she scanned her e-mail and found that Ian had sent a sheaf of photos, she spent half an hour studying the images with an ache in her heart. Soon, this would be all she'd have to remember Rosalie by.

With a twist of anxiety, she returned to the e-mail

program and the ever-growing queue that she'd ignored previously. Since the hospital's Web pages listed her e-mail address, it wasn't unusual to hear from the public—but so many messages!

You brightened my day, read one from Hong Kong. Many blessings.

What a lovely story, wrote a woman in Australia. Fantastic!

Jennifer relaxed as she flipped through more laudatory messages. No one seemed angry or combative. She responded briefly to as many as possible.

Between tending Rosalie, heating a can of soup for dinner and replying to the e-mails, Jennifer lost track of the hour. When the doorbell rang at 9:10 p.m., it startled her.

Ian.

She must look a mess. She'd spilled soup on her sweater, along with a splatter of Rosalie's formula.

All the same, she couldn't wait to see him.

WOMEN WORE MAKEUP and stylish clothes to attract men, but also as a protective shield, Ian mused. He was glad Jennifer trusted him enough to open the door on her rumpled hair and stained sweatshirt, especially since they came with a welcoming smile.

He felt a twinge of guilt. How would she react when and if he interviewed Rosalie's birth mother? Well, he'd worry about that later.

"Sorry I'm late," he said.

"At least you got here, which gives you a better track record than Esther. She didn't bother to show up for the shopping trip we scheduled at her convenience." She reached over to brush a crumb from his collar. "Crackers for dinner?"

That was embarrassing. "With peanut butter. For protein."

"Ah, health food." Jennifer led him through the living room into an office, where she'd set up Rosalie's bassinet. In contrast to the enormous spaces in Mrs. Wycliff's mansion, this felt like a home.

Inhaling the floral scents, Ian realized how isolated he'd become. While he was growing up, despite the family's frequent moves, his parents had always created a nest for him and Anni. Over dinner, they'd discussed the day's events, and at bedtime, read beloved books aloud. He hadn't missed that domesticity…until now.

He rallied his thoughts. "So this Esther person blew you off?"

"We waited so long we barely had time to try on any dresses. I wouldn't be surprised if she missed the wedding entirely." She sat down in her desk chair.

"I nearly missed my sister's wedding, and I was the best man," Ian admitted, strolling across to peek at the baby. He could have sworn she perked up when she saw him. "My plane was late."

"You didn't arrive early for the rehearsals?"

"Blame my brother-in-law for sending me on assignment at the last minute. I didn't even get a chance to rent a tuxedo. Luckily my dad had a spare."

She glanced at the computer. "About your story…"

Ian braced for trouble, although he couldn't imagine what she might object to. "Oh?"

Instead of accessing Flash News/Global's home page,

however, she displayed an e-mail queue. "You won't believe how many readers I've heard from. Listen to this."

He pulled up a chair. "Angry? Disdainful?"

"Quite the opposite."

He leaned forward to read the first one she opened, from a woman in South Africa. Recently, I've been overcome by hopelessness. It seems like nobody cares about one another anymore. You restored my faith in humanity.

"She got all that from my article?"

"I didn't expect this kind of reaction, either." Jennifer clicked on another one, from New Zealand.

Wishing you and your hospital the best of luck. But then, you medical folks work miracles every day, don't you? it read.

"This seems to have touched a lot of people." Ian rarely heard from the public directly; when he did, it was usually to protest some controversy. "Whoever coined the term *human interest* wasn't kidding."

"Some are from parents hoping to adopt. None who live around here, though, and I doubt Orange County's going to start exporting babies." Jennifer shut down the computer. "So what did you do today?"

"Have you heard about the investigation of that federal judge in L.A.?"

"I saw an item in the paper." Sleepily, she swayed toward him.

Ian scooted his chair closer. "Shoulder to lean on, if you want." At this close range, his senses tingled with awareness.

She straightened. "Thanks, but I'm fine. You were telling me about the judge?"

Ian gathered his thoughts. "His ex-wife made some interesting revelations." He proceeded to outline the interview, with Jennifer prompting him at key moments. In the retelling, the judge's shady antics sounded almost comical, save for the impact on the daughter.

"I saw Judge Wycliff at a charity fundraiser once. He seemed dignified, but a little pompous. Guess he didn't look so pompous in his, er, extracurricular poses," Jennifer observed wryly.

Ian chuckled. "I'd love to see his reaction when this story breaks."

"Me, too." She shielded a yawn behind her hand. "Oh, dear. It isn't the company. I'm afraid I'm the early-to-bed type."

Even though he'd prefer to ply her with coffee so they could spend more time talking, he had come to help, Ian recalled. "I'll take the first shift with the baby. I hardly ever turn in before two or three in the morning, anyway."

"That would be wonderful."

After they transferred Rosalie and her gear to the nursery, he brought up his netbook. "I've never used this in a rocking chair before. Ought to be interesting."

"It was kind of you to volunteer." Jennifer touched his cheek. Alarming how powerfully his body responded, although he hoped she didn't notice. "I'm sure you'd rather be enjoying the Hollywood nightlife."

No, I'd rather be kissing you. "One nightclub's pretty much like another anywhere in the world. But I don't know anywhere else quite like here."

"Like what? My messy apartment?"

"I'm not sure what I meant," Ian admitted.

As she leaned over the crib, he saw again that trace

of sadness he'd noticed the previous night. Someone ought to love this woman and have children with her, to banish that expression forever. Someone who could be happy living an ordinary life in a quiet town like Safe Harbor.

Someone very different from Ian.

"'Night. I'll come in later, I promise." With a hint of a smile, she disappeared down the hall.

A few minutes later, Ian heard the shower running. Sudsy water, streaming over her slim body, her gently rounded breasts, her...

Get your head somewhere else. He'd better confine his fantasies to the idea of taking over "From the Fire." In case his superiors quizzed him about his plans, he intended to have a whole sheaf of proposals ready.

Ian opened his computer. It took several tries to find a comfortable position, but finally he angled his long legs to support the machine as he read through Armand Ephron's recent pieces. Brilliant work on inside stories from Asia, Africa and Eastern Europe. A replacement would need to put his own stamp on the column, but how?

Widen the focus, Ian mused. South America didn't receive nearly as much coverage as it should. Neither did controversial medical issues. Who said politics and war were the only topics worth writing about?

He continued reading, moving on to a couple of magazines he subscribed to online and studying them for trends and possibilities. As he worked, he had a sense of the night gathering around him. Outside noises faded. Inside, a floor lamp bathed him in its cozy cheer.

After a while, Rosalie's eyes popped open, but when she started to fuss, Ian sang an old drinking song he'd learned in France. She settled back, apparently oblivious to his atrocious accent.

When he was sure she'd fallen asleep, he removed a spare set of overnight gear from his bag and went to the spare bathroom to brush his teeth. Returning to the rocking chair, he allowed himself to relax.

Someday maybe he'd have a home like this. Once he'd made his mark. Once he'd fulfilled the burning need that had powered him since his teen years to explore the world and challenge himself. To be the reporter others admired, the war-scarred veteran whose rare appearance at a college seminar drew packed crowds. The man who dug deep into the human soul, and found his own at the same time.

Although peripherally aware of his surroundings, Ian must have dozed. A noise woke him—a soft keening. Springing to his feet, he went to the crib, but the baby's little face was tranquil.

He heard it again, a faint sob, and pinpointed the source as Jennifer's room down the hall. What had happened to disturb her so profoundly?

Ian was trying to figure out whether to respond when he heard her cry out, "Where is he? What have you done with my baby?"

Then she screamed. He broke into a run.

Chapter Nine

Jennifer awoke in a man's arms. Tender, strong arms that pulled her out of the wrenching terror of her dream. For an instant, she didn't know where she was, and the only reality became the stroking of her hair and the hard chest beneath her cheek.

Her body trembled to the racing of her heart. Her baby…gone…no one to comfort her…but there *was* someone, this man who'd slid into bed beside her and gathered her close. Safe in his protection, she released her loss and loneliness in a sigh.

"Nightmare?" It was Ian's voice.

In the darkness, she nodded against his solid support.

"I had a few of those after I got shot," he said.

"You were shot?"

"In Iraq, during an interview. Afterward, I let people think it didn't faze me, but my dreams knew better."

Jennifer understood about covering up your pain. Even now, she regretted crying out as she emerged from sleep, although she was grateful Ian had come. "This hasn't happened in years." She struggled to a sitting position. "I'm not usually so…emotional."

He sat up, too, and plumped the extra pillow behind him. As her eyes adjusted to the dimness, she saw that his shirt had come untucked and his sleeves were rolled up. "It sounded like you were trying to find a baby," Ian said quietly.

How much had she revealed? "I don't remember...."

"Did you give one up for adoption?"

He was too damn perceptive. Jennifer never talked about this, never. Only her mother knew the whole story, and Mimi's life was in such perpetual turmoil that she'd probably put it right out of her mind.

"Worse," she said. "He died." Her voice broke.

"You don't have to talk about it." Ian drew the covers over them. "I could just hold you."

Her pulse slowed. "You're here to watch over Rosalie, not me."

"I'm here to make sure you rest. Maybe spilling this will help." His rich voice reverberated like a cello. "Tell you what. I'll show you my scar if you'll show me yours."

His teasing note lightened her mood—and besides, he'd piqued her curiosity. "What kind of scar?"

"From the bullet wound. Got a flashlight?"

"Ian, I can turn on the lamp." Jennifer supposed she should skip this whole silly business, but she couldn't resist. Tomorrow, he'd be gone, and in a week or so he'd leave the region entirely. She doubted she'd ever see him again, let alone share another moment like this.

Which meant she'd never have to face him and feel embarrassed, either.

"I promised to show you my scar. Not my stubbly

face." Amusement rippled through the words. "Besides, I like feeling as if we're holed up in some remote place, just you and me."

Keeping the world at bay. Yes, she liked that idea, too.

In the bedside table, Jennifer found a flashlight. Ian unbuttoned his shirt and bared his left shoulder. "There."

She trained the beam on him and spotted a puckered indentation. "It's smaller than I expected."

"Got a better one." Shrugging his arm from the sleeve, he turned his back to her. "Check out the exit wound."

It was larger and more irregular. "How did this happen? Were you embedded with troops?" Instinctively, her finger traced the jagged shape. Beneath her touch, his skin quivered. "I'm sorry. Does that hurt?"

"No, it's…kind of nice. I was interviewing a faction leader in the middle of Baghdad. Stray bullet. Missed the vital organs. No wonder people say I'm lucky."

She caught the tension in his voice. "What aren't you telling me?" Suddenly uneasy, she removed her finger.

"Leave your hand there. Feels good. No one's touched it since the medic stitched me up."

Without thinking, Jennifer bent and kissed the mark. "All better."

He laughed. "Okay, I showed you mine."

"Finish your story." With the cover tented around them, she really did feel as if they were huddled far from civilization.

Ian slid his shirt back into place. "Not much to tell. I was young and stupid. The wound looked small, so I stuck a scarf over it to stem the bleeding and finished the interview. Later, the medic said I could have bled to death. That's when I got scared."

"Surely it hurt!" She couldn't imagine ignoring a bullet wound.

"Like acid poured on fire. I considered it a badge of honor to gut my way through it."

"Men can be such chowder heads." Jennifer switched off the flashlight.

"Your turn."

"My turn to—?"

"Spill," he reminded her.

She gathered her courage. Well, she had promised, and what a relief to be able to talk, here in the darkness. "I was seventeen. My boyfriend, Frank, was two years older. He…" How much of the story to pour out? Just the part about the baby. *One wound at a time.* "We were driving…we lost control and crashed. I was five months pregnant. The baby died. The doctor said that at least I could have more, as if that made it all right."

"What happened to Frank?"

"Long gone." No sense dwelling on him. "I named the baby Edward, after my father, Eduardo Serra."

"How'd he take it?"

The question puzzled her, and then she registered that Ian was referring to her father. "My parents divorced when I was three and Dad dropped out of my life. He didn't know about his grandson."

She felt a light kiss on her temple. "I'm sorry," Ian murmured. "Men have really let you down, haven't they?"

"Sometimes." She didn't want to nurse her old anger, especially not this evening. On the bed, she angled toward Ian. Wanting, and not wanting, his mouth to close over hers. And then it did.

He paused, as if giving her a chance to protest. Perhaps she ought to stop him, but the contact felt right. Necessary. Gripping his shoulders to steady herself, she teased his lips with her tongue, inviting more.

His palms slid along her silky nightgown, caressing her waistline. Jennifer's body tingled.

Releasing her from a long kiss, Ian cupped her face and studied her. In the dimness, she saw a question in his eyes, and then he lifted her nightgown, his hand tracing the curve of her waist and the swell of her bosom.

Her breasts tightened beneath his thumb and her pulse beat faster. Sensations blossomed inside her.

"Touch me," Ian whispered.

Jennifer spread her hands across his bare chest, relishing its roughness, treasuring the sharp intake of his breath. Tonight they'd taken refuge in each other from their private wars. Tonight, they were healing each other's wounds.

She shrugged off her gown. It caught around her arms, and with a low noise that was half groan and half laughter, Ian's mouth traced the vulnerable naked swell of her breasts before he lifted the fabric free. Together they peeled off his jeans.

"Let me look at you." His body rubbed hers, striking sparks as he eased her down. Then he reached past her. Found the flashlight and discovered her with a beam. "Incredible. I knew your skin would be velvet, but I didn't picture all this." He bent to nip lightly at the inside of her thigh.

Fire flashed through Jennifer. "Let's…" But his mouth reached hers, hushing the words.

The beam shut off. Yet he seemed to be searching for

something in the bedside drawer. He lifted his head. "Don't you have any…? Ah. Found it."

She scarcely remembered buying the condoms. Left from a boyfriend months ago, briefly exciting, quickly gone. As for his name…that was gone, too.

Ian. That name wouldn't leave her soon, even if the man did. But she refused to waste time fretting.

"Could you hurry?" Jennifer asked.

"That's what I like—a woman who knows what she wants." He unrolled the protection. "You're sure you want to do this? I caught you at a vulnerable moment."

"That's the best kind."

"Good point."

As he fitted the sheath, she relished the sight of his lean build. The nightmare had left a void that she needed him to fill. To make her body forget that it had ever held anything but him.

"I'm an honorable man," Ian added. "Most of the time, anyway. So if you aren't sure…"

"Are we going to chitchat all night?" Jennifer teased.

"Hell, no." In an instant, he straddled her, his hardness pressing into her yielding femininity. With restrained power, he parted her and joined them. A wave of bliss rolled through her, pure, hot and insatiable.

Anchoring herself to his hips, Jennifer rocked against him. "Make me whole, Ian," she whispered. "Just for tonight."

Ian thrust slowly. "You can't tell me you don't want this more than once."

"I want a lot more. Right now."

"Oh, man." His rhythm sped up. Jennifer clasped him, because if she didn't hold on tight, she might melt into liquid silver. His mouth and his tongue found hers, and they fused into one being, glorious and free.

Joy claimed her. *Never let this end. Never let me go.*

And he didn't. Afterward, he lay cradling her, his warmth all around, his contentment whispered. The nightmare had passed, and the dream had come.

For tonight.

IAN AWOKE IN A POOL of sunlight. Lazily, he reached across the sheets for the woman who'd tantalized and fulfilled him.

Cool bed. Empty. What the hell?

He sat up, confused. The clock read nearly 8:00 a.m. How had he'd slept this late and where was he supposed to be?

Sunday. He wasn't scheduled to be anywhere.

From down the hall came the rippling sound of Jennifer talking to the baby. Of course. Rosalie required attention.

Relieved, Ian leaned back against the headboard. He'd love a rematch of last night's encounter. Intense and thrilling, it had gone by too fast. Today should offer a leisurely chance to explore each other, but he hadn't considered the requirements of motherhood.

Temporary motherhood. Still, Jennifer had been hurting bad last night, haunted by her trauma. She'd wanted their lovemaking as much as he had, but she also wanted a child. And she had one. Why didn't she seem eager to make the situation permanent?

Well, that was her business.

He closed his eyes, inhaling the luxury of simply being here. Picturing the faintly exotic tilt to her eyes, recalling her unexpected boldness, wondering why he got the sense that last night had been more than a simple, mutually satisfying encounter.

There'd been a moment, or maybe a whole series of moments, when he'd broken through his isolation and truly connected with her. Lost himself. Found himself. What the hell was that all about?

Uncoiling from the bed, Ian went into the bathroom. What a hit of femininity! Nightgown hanging from a peg, cosmetics on the counter, their mingled scent perfuming the air. He might almost be inside her again.

He smiled, contrasting these cozy quarters with other places where he'd cleaned up over the years. Military barracks had been the high point; open-doored stalls the norm; rusty spigots in alleys the occasional last resort. If he landed the "From the Fire" column, his future would hold a lot more of those. Not an appealing prospect at this moment.

In the shower, hot water sheeted off his skin. He wished Jennifer were snuggled in here with him. Maybe Viktor and Anni had the right idea, after all.

Yeah, as if this would last. A few weeks of running tame and he'd be foaming at the mouth.

His shower finished, Ian wrapped a towel around his hips, scooped his dirty clothes off the floor and went down the hall to the baby's room.

Jennifer stood with her back to him at the changing table, brown hair tumbling around her shoulders. She'd thrown on a Chinese-style silk robe that set off her dark coloring and clung to the delicious contours of her body.

She turned, blinking as she took in his state of undress. "You're quite a sight."

Ian grabbed his bag off the floor. "Thought I'd put on some fresh clothes. How's the little one?"

"Fine, thank goodness." She shook back her hair. "So much for our plan to keep an eye on her all night."

He'd forgotten about that. "My intentions were good. Guess I'm not used to parental duties."

"Get dressed, soldier. You're on baby duty now," she replied. "My turn to hit the shower."

"Fair enough. I'll hurry."

After pulling on his spare jeans and shirt, Ian ducked into the bathroom to give his face a once-over with the razor and run a comb through his hair. Back in the nursery, Jennifer transferred Rosalie into his arms.

What a tiny bundle, yet when the little girl blinked up at him trustingly, she became the center of his universe. "I hope I didn't let you down last night," Ian said.

"Are you kidding? You were transcendent," Jennifer responded.

She obviously assumed he'd been talking to her. And he had no intention of correcting that impression. "Transcendent, huh?"

She touched a rough place on his jaw. "You missed a spot."

"Sorry." He ducked his head. "I could give it another once-over."

"Don't bother. It's cute." She backed off. "Help yourself to breakfast."

"Will do."

As he carried the baby downstairs, Ian's jaw tingled from her touch. The casual intimacy of the gesture reminded him once again of his sister and Viktor. The first time he'd stayed with them after their marriage, he'd been struck by how comfortable these two independent beings had become around each other, communicating with a look, conversing in shorthand.

The change in his career-obsessed sister had puzzled him. Now he understood. Even envied her a little.

As he situated the baby and bassinet in a corner of the kitchen, he glanced out at the condo's private patio. Morning light illuminated a flower bed bursting with colors. What a peaceful place to sit side by side, sharing a morning newspaper.

Jennifer had created an oasis. She hadn't given the impression of being the clingy sort, but it occurred to Ian that their lovemaking might have created expectations. Much as he enjoyed this respite, he wasn't seriously tempted to stay here. In case she'd begun to hope for something more, he owed her a warning.

He set the table, started the coffee and made toast, sprinkling cayenne on his to give it bite. "Great selection of jams and jellies," he said when Jennifer entered, fresh and glowing in a knit top and slim pants.

"Seems like every conference or seminar I attend, they give us a selection of these as a souvenir." She inspected a miniature jar. "Mango. Think I'll try that."

"I found some coffee flavorings in the pantry, too, but I take mine straight," Ian said.

"So do I, usually. Those were gifts, too." After peeking at the baby, she swung back toward him. "I hadn't pictured you as the domestic type."

Her remark surprised him. "I'm not."

"Oh?" She indicated the table and coffeepot. "This is nice. I appreciate it. Maybe I'm jumping the gun, but…"

Uh-oh. "I was afraid you might…"

"In case you were assuming…"

They both stopped. "Ladies first," Ian offered, although his sister would have popped him one for uttering anything so sexist.

"I didn't mean to take advantage of you last night," she began.

"Uh—anytime," he said, puzzled.

Jennifer added a tub of butter to the table. "Something came over me, and there you were. It was great. But emotionally, I'm not available. Too many bad choices in the past to risk making them again. I'm happy here, making my own home. Not that I can't share. For a little while. You'll be off then, and that's fine. No lingering ties. In case you planned on any."

Whoa. If he understood correctly, she was blowing *him* off. "Is this what's called letting me down easy?"

Sliding into a seat, she kept her face averted, but he could have sworn she was turning pink. "Something like that."

Ian had no idea what to say. He fiddled with the toaster, examined far more pots of jam than he had any intention of eating, and stirred sweetener into his coffee, although he preferred it bitter.

"You're upset," Jennifer said.

"I shouldn't be. I was going to tell you basically the same thing," he blurted.

"You were?"

Their gazes met across the breakfast table. "I'm being considered for a post I'd give anything for," Ian said. "My own column, my own agenda. Lots of travel, possibly long periods spent with a subject, exploring in-depth. I'm in no position to nurture a relationship."

Her eyebrow quirked. "'Nurture a relationship.' Is that polite-speak for 'Put up with a sex-starved PR lady?'"

He nearly choked on his toast. After a sip of coffee, he replied, "Actually, I'm rather taken with the sex-starved PR lady. I'm just not, as you put it, emotionally available, either."

"Well, that's a relief."

It ought to be. So why wasn't it?

They ate for a while in an edgy silence. Finally Ian ventured a joke. "I must say, your rejection has wounded me to the quick."

"Not used to it, eh?" Jennifer teased.

"I'm only half kidding."

"Which half?"

Good question. "The half that really likes you," he admitted.

"It's unfortunate that we're so similar." She regarded him thoughtfully. "In some ways, we're exactly right for each other. I mean, in the sense of being people who need our distances, but need each other sometimes, too."

"We could have both," he said, and then wondered what on earth had impelled him to suggest that.

"Long-distance relationship?" Jennifer's mouth twisted wryly.

"Wouldn't work," he conceded. "But I do get posted to L.A. occasionally. Think you could put up with me a few times a year?" Or more, if he worked it right.

"I can't make any promises," she warned.

"Maybe you'll fall in love with some doctor." He wasn't sure why he'd thrown that in. "Isn't that every woman's dream?"

"Not mine."

"Why not?"

She shrugged. "It's too awkward, dating people at work. I did that once on a previous job. The breakup was miserable."

"You had to face him day after day?" he ventured.

"No, he switched to another office, but I had to put up with people feeling sorry for me." Obviously, that didn't suit her. Strong-minded woman.

Ian's cell rang. For once, he'd love to turn it off, but he couldn't. Especially not with the "From the Fire" position on the line. "Ian Martin," he answered.

It was Pierre. After excusing himself from the table, Ian moved to the living room.

The photographer had a short but succinct piece of information. It not only changed Ian's plans for the day, it changed a whole lot more.

Possibly even the way he felt about Jennifer.

Chapter Ten

When Ian returned to the kitchen, Jennifer saw the tightness in his expression. "Bad news?"

"You might say that."

Her stomach lurched. Why did she get the impression he was angry with her? "What happened?"

Folding his arms, he leaned against the counter. "Pierre just heard on the radio that two babies were relinquished at your hospital today. It seems they aren't alone. Three more were given up yesterday. I guess this explains your sudden invitation for me to spend the day following you around."

She'd almost forgotten about that. Jennifer's next thought was, *I hope he hasn't found out about the cousins.* "That's it?" she ventured.

"Is there more?"

She should have kept her mouth shut. Well, she'd just have to wing this. "I didn't know about today's relinquishments, and whoever leaked this to the press has a lot to answer for."

"But you knew about yesterday's."

Might as well own up, as far as she dared. "Yes. I'm

sorry, Ian. I had to try to keep a lid on things. Just as, I might point out, you had to interview Samantha whether I liked it or not."

His regretful gaze met hers. "Point taken. I see what you mean about not dating coworkers. Or frenemies, as the case may be."

Friendly enemies. "Is that what I am?"

"I wish that weren't the case. But I suppose so."

Five minutes ago, she'd been straining to keep Ian at arm's length. All the same, his withdrawal stung. Nothing she could do about it. "I'd better get over to the hospital. In full battle mode." Rising, Jennifer began clearing away the remnants of breakfast.

"Planning to take down the big mouth in your camp?" He gave her a crooked grin.

"That, and manage the press." She shuddered at the prospect of fending off swarms of reporters. "I'd better call Dr. Rayburn, in case he hasn't heard."

"Before you do…" Any sign of humor vanished from his expression. "I'm not obligated to warn you about this, but I will, anyway."

His strained tone froze her. "What is it, Ian?"

"Viktor asked me to find Sunny and interview her about Rosalie. Much as I hate raking all that up, I have to do it."

"What about her right to privacy?"

"I can't let the rest of the media get ahead of me."

"Especially not with a promotion on the line," she retorted. Seeing him flinch, she backtracked. "That was unfair. We both have obligations."

Ian cast a wistful glance at the baby, who lay taking in this interchange with cheerful innocence. "I'm going to miss you guys."

And I'm going to try like hell not to miss you. "See you at the med center." Jennifer sponged off the table. The last thing she wanted to see when she came home were reminders of their time together.

"If there's anything I can... Never mind. It's not like you'd trust me behind the scenes again, would you?" Abruptly, Ian strode out. As she loaded the dishwasher, Jennifer heard his footsteps on the stairs. She followed his movements from the creaking ceiling as he collected his stuff and descended. "Well, I'm off."

"Bye." Her throat thick with emotion, she barely squeezed out the word.

He paused. "I'll pass along one more tip, or rather, suspicion. Before you go running off to cross-examine the duty nurses about the leak, don't overlook the obvious suspect."

"I'm sorry?"

"Ask yourself who might *want* the press to cover this." With a mock salute, Ian spun and exited. The air pressure seemed to funnel out in his wake.

When his meaning hit her, she wished it hadn't. *Samantha.* She'd already alienated a man she cared about much more than she should. Now she might have to antagonize one of her few, precious friends.

First, though, she put in the obligatory call to Mark. The administrator took a fatalistic approach. "Bound to happen sooner or later," he said. "I'll meet you there."

"See you in a few." She didn't mention the possibility that Sam might be involved. Her friend deserved better.

Postponing the call, Jennifer got the baby ready to go. This would be tricky, managing the infant along with work, but the employee day-care center didn't operate on Sundays.

Under other circumstances, she might have asked her friends to help. But by the end of the day, she wasn't sure she would have any left.

IAN ENTERED THE HOSPITAL lobby behind a young man accompanied by a pregnant woman. A flash went off, and half a dozen people wearing press IDs descended on the hapless couple.

Idiots. The woman wasn't relinquishing a baby; she hadn't even given birth yet. And she wore a wedding ring. "Did we win something?" asked her husband.

A security guard intervened. "I have to ask you folks to step aside," he told the reporters. "You can't be bothering our clients."

"Miss Serra's on her way," Ian informed him briskly. "She sent me ahead. Thanks for handling this."

"Just doing my job, sir," the man said.

While the couple signed in at the desk, Ian strode toward the elevators. None of the other reporters ratted him out. Professional courtesy, or else they just didn't think fast enough.

After exiting on the fifth floor, he put in a call to Pierre. Never mind the signs about not using cell phones. He doubted the administrative offices housed sensitive medical equipment.

"I'm on the 405 Freeway," the photographer said. "ETA half an hour."

Ian advised him about the situation in the lobby. "Why

don't you stake it out in case more babies show up? Now that I made it past the gendarmes, I plan to skulk."

"You sure got there fast," Pierre observed.

Ian let the silence stretch too long, because his brain refused to spit out any credible excuses.

"Oh, man," the photographer said. "You didn't."

"She blindsided me," Ian told him.

"I hope she's good in bed, at least."

The best. "We played dominoes all night and kept an eye on the baby."

"Yeah, right."

He was clicking off when a door opened from the administrative suite. A blonde girl, face streaked with tears, came out, followed by a guy in a suit jacket over jeans. Tony Franco, Ian recalled.

"Thanks for filling out the paperwork." The attorney caught sight of Ian and stiffened. "You're not supposed to be here."

Ian held up his hands. "Just need to ask you something."

"Wait here." The man accompanied the young mother down the hall, bypassing the main elevators. There must be others that led to a rear exit.

Tony returned. "How'd you get past the guard?"

"Smoke and mirrors."

"Guess you're better at this than the local press." The man cleared his throat. "What's the question?"

"I need to find Sunny. Rosalie's mother."

"That isn't a question."

"Okay. Where is she?"

"Can't tell you."

He'd figured as much. "Will you at least tell me her last name?"

"Seeing as you're such a brilliant reporter, I'll let you find that out for yourself," Tony said.

"Isn't her identity a matter of public record?"

"In your dreams." The man regarded him with mock friendliness. "Anything else I can *not* help you with?"

Even though the joke came at his own expense, Ian couldn't help chuckling. "Not at the moment, counselor."

"It being Sunday, I think I'll take myself home."

"How can you be sure no one else will relinquish a baby?"

"I've left instruction with the staff. I'm sure they can handle it." Giving him a brief wave, the attorney ambled off.

Ian stood debating how to proceed. He refused to return to the lobby and give up the advantage of having bluffed his way past the guards. Besides, Pierre could cover any new arrivals.

Come to think of it, Rosalie likely shared her mother's surname, and he felt certain Jennifer had paperwork to go with the baby. Damn. He refused to try to trick her into revealing that information, and he could hardly expect her to cooperate. Where did that leave him?

With a breaking story to report about surrendered babies in need of homes. Surely the staff at the nursery could at least advise him of the infants' conditions and voice their personal reactions to the influx. That ought to satisfy Flash News/Global's readers for the moment.

But not for long.

ENTERING THROUGH THE EMPLOYEES' door to avoid the media, Jennifer tried to focus on the tasks ahead, yet her mind kept rebelling.

She couldn't let her feelings for Ian show when she faced him in the presence of others. Had to maintain this collected exterior she'd strained so hard to develop over the years. *You can't trust him or your own judgment. Arm's length. That's the key—arm's length.*

No more private conversations over her kitchen table, let alone escapades in the bedroom. *Only that wasn't an escapade. It was precious.*

And never to be repeated.

The grumble of voices from the lobby reached Jennifer even before she peeked in from the corridor. Nearly a dozen reporters and photographers milled in a corner, watched by a guard who clearly took his duties very seriously. From this angle, she recognized Pierre but saw no sign of Ian.

She didn't kid herself that he'd simply left. He was no doubt in the building and up to mischief.

From the cafeteria, Mark scooted toward her, also keeping out of view of the media. "Got a call right after yours, from Ms. Yashimoto in Louisville," he said quietly. "Word spreads fast. She seems to think we ought to try to quash this whole business."

"That would be a mistake," Jennifer advised. "The best we can do is spin it to our advantage."

"Agreed." The administrator studied her sympathetically. "Where's the baby, if you don't mind my asking?"

"Samantha's watching her so I could work." Jennifer hoped he didn't notice the heat spreading to her cheeks.

She'd hated having to call her friend and ask whether she'd been the source of the leak.

Anyone else might have taken offense, but Samantha had explained calmly that she respected the young women's privacy too much to blab to reporters, and was glad Jennifer had prevented her from saying too much to Ian yesterday. Then she'd offered to watch Rosalie for a few hours.

Jennifer had never had a girlfriend that generous. She wasn't even sure she deserved one, after she'd practically accused Samantha of...well, indiscretion.

"I'm glad she's staying home. I hope this means Sam's going to give us a break," Mark said. "Her heart's in the right place, but we can't afford to operate as a charitable institution."

"I'm sure she understands the issues."

"She's passionate and idealistic." The obstetrician shook his head admiringly. "Like I used to be before I grew up. Oh, never mind that. You're the expert in this situation. What's our next step?"

"Finding the leak," Jennifer said. *And catching Ian before he turns the leak into a flood.*

"Do you suppose some publicity-happy mother called it in herself?" Mark suggested.

If so, the woman would probably be preening in front of the media, and Jennifer hadn't seen anyone doing that. "I'm betting on the staff. We should start with the nursery—diplomatically, of course. I'd be happy to handle it."

"Thanks." His dark eyebrows formed a thick line. "I'd rather not hurt morale by interrogating the staff myself. Now, what can I do?"

"You could talk to the reporters. They need information about exactly how many babies we've taken in, how they're being cared for and what's next for them. If you like, I'll help you prepare a statement."

"Excellent. You look for the leak while I pull the data together."

What a pleasure to work with a boss who acted like a colleague rather than a taskmaster. "That would be great. We should be ready to issue a statement within an hour."

"Gotcha."

At the third-floor nursery level, Jennifer stepped out, while Mark continued up to his office. As the doors closed behind her, she saw Ian.

Her breath caught in her chest. That rumpled hair, the familiar planes of his face. She fought back the urge to reach out to him.

When he spotted her, he broke off his earnest conversation with a red-haired girl in a volunteer's smock. "Ms. Serra. Glad you could join us." His mouth quirked in a wry welcome.

She noted the name on the girl's clip-on bar. "Judi, you shouldn't be talking to Mr. Martin. He's a member of the media."

Freckles stood out as the volunteer flushed. "I'm really sorry. I didn't mean to do it."

"Do what?"

"When I saw the new babies coming in this morning, I called my cousin at the *L.A. Times*. I was just trying to do him a favor. Then I got to talking with Ian—Mr. Martin—a few minutes ago, and he said I…I breached the patients' rights or something." Tears glistened on Judi's cheeks. "I never thought about that."

Jennifer wondered how much information Ian had extracted before he chose to take the high road. Still, she appreciated his assistance. Now she had to decide how to proceed.

"I'm sure you didn't mean any harm, but our patients deserve protection, not exploitation. How would you feel if you had to give up a baby and someone spread it all over the news?" she scolded.

The girl hugged herself, misery plain on her face. "Please don't kick me out. I want to be a physical therapist and I need this volunteer job for my college résumé. I'll scrub floors or change bedpans or anything."

How could she not sympathize? "I'll recommend that you be reassigned to the cafeteria for the rest of this school year," Jennifer told her. "Right now, though, you should go home. By the rear exit, please."

"Thank you!" Judi's mouth trembled. "I feel so stupid."

"We all make mistakes." *I made a much bigger one when I was your age.*

"I'll go get my stuff. No more big mouth. I promise." The girl broke into a trot down the hallway.

Beyond her, through the large window, row after row of bassinets caught Jennifer's attention. Most of the infants, of course, belonged to patients, but some of them must have been relinquished. Babies just like Rosalie.

Her heart squeezed. Tomorrow, she had to come back here and hand her child to a social worker. How was it possible never to see Rosalie again, perhaps never even to learn where she'd been placed or whether she was happy?

"You look like you're about to cry." Although Ian

moved closer, he stopped short of touching her. No doubt aware, as she was, that they stood in full view of a passing orderly, the duty nurses and any patients or visitors who might wander by.

"I'm fine."

"You were kind to that girl," he said.

She forced herself to regard Ian straight on, and nearly got lost in his deep blue gaze. "I'm not heartless."

"I can attest to that."

A foolish urge swept over her, to take his hand and lead him out of this place. To spend the rest of the day alone with him and Rosalie, living in a fantasy.

Instead, she replied, "Now that you've found my loose cannon, I have to help Dr. Rayburn prepare a press release. By the way, did Judi tell you anything that ought to be confidential?"

"Just a few quotes about how cute the babies are and how healthy they seem," he assured her.

She wondered how he'd accomplished so easily a task that might have taken hours. "How did you discover she was the leak?"

"She practically bragged about it. Kids today seem to think anything that happens is fair game to broadcast." Ian had the grace to look abashed. "I can't imagine what gave them that idea."

"People like you?" she joked.

He pretended to duck. "Ouch. By the way, I'm glad I was wrong about Dr. Forrest being the source. Hope that didn't create problems for you."

"Quite the contrary. She volunteered to babysit." That didn't mean the incident might not bother Samantha later, but there was nothing to be done about that. "I'm afraid I'll have to escort you to the lobby, Mr. Flash News/Global."

"I understand." A familiar ring tone sounded. "Excuse me." He took out his cell. "Ian Martin."

Jennifer bit back an instinctive objection. No sense scolding him for using it inside the hospital, since she was ousting him from the treatment floors, anyway.

"Who? Oh! *Sunny,*" he said into the phone. "Thanks for returning my call. Did you see the article I wrote about your daughter yesterday? Good. Any chance I could interview you? There's a lot of interest internationally."

Everything else flew out of Jennifer's mind. He'd gotten hold of Rosalie's mother. What if Sunny had changed her mind about keeping her daughter?

You intended to give her up, anyway. Somehow, that thought failed to provide comfort.

"Sure, I could fill you in about how she's doing. In fact, I just saw her this morning," Ian went on. "I'd be glad to come to your place…. You sure you can't do it today? No, no, tomorrow will be fine. You want to see her? Well, I don't know… Sure, if you insist. You still have legal rights, I gather."

The lights seemed to dim. Sunny had decided to reenter the picture. That might turn out to be best for Rosalie, but a blow for Jennifer.

Because no matter how hard she tried to lie to herself, she'd just come face-to-face with the agonizing truth that she'd given her heart to this baby, and handing her to someone else meant losing a child she loved all over again.

Chapter Eleven

On Monday morning, as he waited for Sunny in the hospital conference room, Ian was keenly aware of all those who *weren't* present.

Pierre, for instance. His subject had refused to permit cameras.

More importantly, Jennifer. She'd called a few minutes ago to say Rosalie had required a last-minute diaper change, so they'd be late. She'd sounded way beyond tense, as if perched on the edge of a cliff, straining to keep from falling.

He'd seen the anguish in her expression yesterday when she heard him talking to Sunny. Despite her professional air, he'd instantly caught the message.

She loved that little girl. Maybe she'd already decided to seek an adoption. Now, thanks to Ian's interference, the mother might change her mind and keep the baby.

Regret clouded his gaze as he stared through the window, over the four-story medical building next door and the geometric layout of offices and apartments beyond. Seemed like he couldn't help hurting Jennifer, despite his best intentions. In his years of reporting, he'd slept with a few women he'd met through stories, but he'd never had reason to worry about them afterward.

Jennifer had declared flat out that she didn't want any ties, yet he felt a responsibility toward her. Maybe it was the sense he kept getting of her vulnerability, bordering on fragility. Did it stem from her long-ago miscarriage? Or was there more that she hadn't told him?

Well, she had a right to her secrets. And he had an obligation to do his job.

He'd found Sunny's last name on the Internet, where an acquaintance had identified her in a blog, and called her listed phone number. He'd left a message, probably one of zillions. She'd returned it, she'd explained, because she'd seen his interview with Jennifer.

Why had she insisted that Jennifer, as well as Rosalie, be present for the interview? Well, he was about to find out.

Through the open doorway drifted low voices. Then Tony glanced inside and gave Ian a nod of recognition. "I gather Jennifer and Mark approved this interview." His tone implied that he didn't agree. "Miss Baron, if you need any help, I'm at your service."

"I'm fine, thanks." The young woman who slipped past him had tied back her hair and replaced her smock with jeans and a tank top. Standing to shake hands, Ian registered the redness around her eyes.

At close range, Sunny appeared older than the sixteen or seventeen he'd first assumed. "Mind if I ask your age?"

The question appeared to startle her. "Twenty. Why?"

"Just assembling the vital statistics." Since she was surveying the room with a frown, he added, "Miss Serra's on the way. Seems there was a diaper emergency."

"So she kept the baby all weekend, like she promised?" Clutching her oversize purse, the girl remained standing.

"She did."

"How are they getting along?"

He decided to be frank since, once Jennifer arrived, he could hardly talk freely about her. "In my opinion, they've bonded. Just as you hoped." When she didn't respond, he decided to drop the subject. It was hardly his place to pressure her one way or another about keeping the baby. "Have a seat and we'll get started. No sense wasting time."

The girl edged into a chair. "I want her to hear my story, too."

Ian took a seat around the corner of the conference table. "You saw her for a few seconds in a video. What made you decide she was the right person to raise your child?"

The young woman's chin came up and she regarded him squarely. In this sudden show of self-possession, Ian glimpsed a strong-mindedness beneath the shy exterior. "She seemed kind. A lot of people are quick to judge me."

"Which people?"

"At the jazz club where I work. They think I'm selfish to give up my baby."

Although he'd quietly switched on his digital recorder, Ian jotted notes as backup. "You figured Jennifer wouldn't judge?"

"She looked like she understands how it feels to get hurt."

"You figured that out from the video?" Amazing.

"I've watched it over and over on my laptop." Sunny

stared down at her hands. "You remember what she said? 'Every day I walk past our nursery and wish I could hold them all in my arms.' Then she started to cry. Yeah, I think at some level she's like me."

"You're right," he said quietly.

Sunny blinked. "How well do you know her, anyway?"

This was dangerous ground. "She gave me a lot of access while I was working on the follow-up story."

A smile broke through the solemnity, and for the first time the name Sunny seemed to fit her. "Is that what you call it? Access?"

He chuckled. "You're pretty perceptive."

"People don't expect that from me."

"Spruce up your image and you'll knock 'em dead," he suggested.

"I might try that."

From the hallway, Ian heard the creak of the baby carriage. Sunny's brightness faded, and she clutched her purse harder.

She was nervous, he realized, and uncertain how she'd react to seeing her baby. A dramatic moment, noted the observant part of Ian's brain. Great stuff for his article. Only he had a hard time enjoying the opportunity. Not that he'd ever been entirely indifferent to his subjects' feelings, but this time, he cared more than he should.

A lot more.

A TWINGE OF FEAR shivered through Jennifer as she faced this young woman who held the future in her hands. Only last Friday, Sunny had been a defenseless stranger and Jennifer the confident professional. Now everything had changed.

At the same time, she couldn't help noting that despite the differences in coloring—Rosalie was blonde and blue-eyed, Sunny had light brown hair and hazel eyes— the pair had the same small ears and generous mouths.

"Hi, Sunny, Ian. Sorry I'm late." Despite her best effort, her voice trembled. Struggling to regain control, Jennifer bent to lift Rosalie from the stroller.

"Wow, what a cute outfit!" Sunny fingered the red sleeper covered with white hearts. "She looks like she's grown already. Is that possible?"

"She's gained four ounces." Samantha had insisted on weighing her. "And that was as of yesterday." Cradling the baby against her shoulder, Jennifer forced herself to ask, "Would you like to hold her?"

Sunny took a deep breath. Behind her, Ian watched them both with an unreadable expression. In reporter mode, Jennifer presumed. She'd have to be careful what she said in front of him.

Yesterday afternoon, after she and Mark finished answering the press's questions, she'd experienced a completely irrational urge to pack up and take Rosalie somewhere, anywhere, that no one could find them. Such a place didn't exist, of course, and besides, Jennifer wouldn't deprive Sunny of her child if the young mother truly wanted her back. Still, the force of her own emotions had shocked her.

And now here she was, prepared to say goodbye. Or, at least, she hoped she could.

Even if it broke her heart.

To her surprise, Sunny folded her arms. "I can't. If I do, I might…well, act stupid, and I've already done more than enough of that already."

Jennifer was flooded with relief. Yet she knew this wasn't over yet. "Would you like me to leave so you can conduct the interview?"

"I asked for you to be here." Sunny plopped into a chair. "Please stay."

Ian shrugged. Apparently, he didn't understand the young woman's motives, either.

"Hold on a minute." After resettling Rosalie in the carriage, Jennifer wheeled it around the table and sat close to Ian so Sunny wouldn't have to keep swiveling her head between them.

His clean male scent teased at her nostrils, and he plucked a receiving blanket from Jennifer's shoulder. "I doubt you meant to wear this all day."

Embarrassed at having overlooked it, and even more by the way she enjoyed his touch, she tucked it in the diaper bag. "Guess I'm a little distracted." She folded her hands on the table and focused on Sunny.

Ian picked up his pad. "Okay. So you're a singer."

"No, just a waitress girl. I'm working my way through community college," Sunny said.

"Any particular field in mind?"

"Accounting. I like numbers." She grimaced. "I got pretty good at counting to nine months. Boy, was I an idiot. You can write that. Go ahead. You won't hurt my feelings. I was really, really dumb."

"Don't be so hard on yourself," Jennifer told her.

Sunny shot Ian an almost gleeful look. "I told you she wouldn't judge!"

"Judge you for what?" Jennifer asked.

"For being selfish about my future. I grew up in foster homes, and since I turned eighteen, I've been on my own. Broke and struggling. I don't want that kind of life for my kid."

"That isn't selfish," Jennifer protested.

"Thank you!"

"What about the father?" Ian asked. "What's his view of all this?"

Jennifer almost wished he hadn't brought that up. But fathers had a lot of legal rights these days. Better to find out the situation now than later.

"You mean Daddy Hit and Run?" Sunny scoffed. "He's married. That's another thing people judge me about, but I honestly didn't know. He didn't wear a ring."

Ian looked up from his notes. "How did you meet him?"

"He drove a tow truck. My car broke down and I didn't know how I was going to pay for repairs. He said he'd fix it free on his own time."

Taking advantage, Jennifer thought. Manipulating a young woman by pretending to be kind.

"After he fixed it, I couldn't very well refuse when he asked me out to dinner," Sunny went on. "One thing led to another. You get the picture."

They'd dated for a couple of months, she explained. Beginning to suspect he might be living with a woman because he never took her to his home, she'd followed him from work.

"Two little kids ran out of the house yelling, 'Daddy! Daddy.' I felt like a total jerk," she said. "And then, guess what? Missed my period. We'd been careless about using protection. Like I said, stupid, stupid, stupid."

"Especially him," Jennifer blurted. "A married man with children already!"

"Exactly." Sunny's head bobbed for emphasis. "I was

scared and angry and a little excited, too. I mean, I knew being pregnant was a miracle, in a way. But not for me, not right then."

Like the stab of a thorn, a long-forgotten moment flashed back. A seventeen-year-old Jennifer leaning against the counter in the bathroom of the mobile home, staring in disbelief at the blue stick. Terrified of telling her mother, wondering what on earth Frank would say, but at the same time thrilled that someone as confused as her could be carrying a new life.

"What happened when you told him?" Ian asked.

For an instant, Jennifer thought he meant Frank. He didn't, of course. But she couldn't help seeing the scene that evening, sitting in her boyfriend's car at a park. A streetlight had picked out the pride and uncertainty on Frank's angular face. "Okay, sweetie," he'd said. "This oughta be interesting."

Clearly, he hadn't been planning ahead. Or, if he was, he'd been planning the wrong things. Too bad she hadn't known that at the time.

"Ron wanted me to get rid of it. When I refused, he wrote me a check for a thousand dollars to help with expenses, along with a handwritten note relinquishing all paternal rights. I gave that to the attorney here." Sunny scowled. "I went to the bank and cashed the check right away. I even had them call his bank to make sure it wouldn't bounce."

"A thousand bucks doesn't go far these days," Ian noted.

Jennifer thought about the cost of medical care and baby equipment. "It's a drop in the bucket."

"I did the best I could." Sunny's eyes misted. "I used low-cost clinics and then an unlicensed midwife. It wasn't safe, but what could I do?"

"You didn't ask Ron for more help?" Ian probed.

"When I stopped by the garage to talk to him, the owner said he'd left. Turns out I wasn't the only girl he'd been fooling around with." Sunny shook her head. "He ran off. Left his wife and kids, too. How did I get involved with a rat like that?"

"He played you," Jennifer told her. "Some guys are good at manipulating women."

"You get it, just like I figured you would." Sunny leaned forward. "You'll keep her, right? You'll adopt Rosalie?"

A great bubble of joy formed inside Jennifer. "You didn't come here to take her back?"

"I wanted to make sure she was okay. And one more thing." Sunny tapped a finger uneasily on the table.

"Anything," Jennifer breathed.

"You love her." It was a statement, not a question.

"More than the whole world."

Sunny gave her a wistful smile. "My other reason for coming today is so you can tell her this story when she grows up. About how much I loved her, how I would have kept her if it had been fair to both of us. As for the part about Ron, maybe you can say he died."

"I don't want to lie. But I'll figure out some way to soften it." Jennifer reached across the table to squeeze Sunny's hand. "That's what I do for a living—put a spin on things."

"Yeah." The young woman swallowed hard. "Now I gotta go." But she left her hand in Jennifer's for a second before withdrawing.

Ian flipped a page in his pad. "What does the future hold for you?"

"Who knows?" When Sunny rose, her figure looked

slimmer than a few days ago. "I'm off. Oh, here's my phone number in case you need me to sign any more papers." She handed over a slip of paper. "Take good care of her."

"Would you like to stay in touch?" Jennifer wasn't sure whether she should offer, but it seemed only reasonable.

"I'd rather make a clean break. I might be moving to Phoenix. My cousin invited me to stay with her, and I could transfer. Don't put that in your story," she told Ian.

"I won't."

After Sunny left, he shut his notepad and turned off the recorder. Jennifer remained in her seat, trying to absorb what had just happened.

She'd committed herself to raising this baby. How wonderful and terrifying.

"You look shell-shocked," Ian commented. "What's running through your head?"

"Off the record?"

He gave a start. "Hey, what kind of jerk do you take me for? Don't answer that. Of course it's off the record. I was trying to make sure you're all right."

Jennifer allowed herself to focus on the roguish smile playing around his mouth. "I missed you last night," she blurted. "Oh, damn. That wasn't what I meant to say."

"For what it's worth, I missed you, too."

She didn't dare explore the subject further. One dream had just come true, and she needed all her energy to come to grips with that. "I'm trying to figure out how I'm going to manage."

"Day care and stuff like that?" he asked.

"The hospital has a day-care center. No, I mean that most women who raise a child have a support system.

A husband, a family, a community where they've lived for a long time. I'm kind of on my own here." Jennifer certainly couldn't turn to her mother, whose sporadic drinking and emotional seesaw made her unreliable.

"Seems to me you have some remarkable friends," Ian observed.

That isn't the same as having you around. Jennifer bit her lip before she could voice anything so foolish. He'd spent a night with her, nothing more.

Men didn't stick around. Not the ones she picked.

"Yes, I do have friends, and enough love to sustain my daughter and me." The word *daughter* gave her a thrill.

"I believe you." Ian seemed in no hurry to leave the conference room. "Sunny had you pegged, just from watching the video."

"Pegged how?"

"She figured out that you'd been wounded, that you'd suffered a loss." He spoke with a trace of huskiness. "She also knew you wouldn't judge her."

How could I judge her, when I've done so much worse? She hadn't told him everything, though, and there was no point in doing so now. Instead, Jennifer said, "Thank you, Ian."

He frowned. "For what?"

She'd asked the attorney's opinion about that earlier. "Since the father relinquished his rights and I have the mother's permission, all I have to do is pass a home study with a social worker to make sure I can keep the baby safe and provide for her. Tony said that under the circumstances it's okay to have Rosalie already home with me until we can change that. Then I'll need a judge's approval, but once I pass the home study, that should be automatic."

"Are you sure the social workers will let you keep her?"

"I don't see how they can refuse. She isn't their case yet, and I have the birth mother's support," Jennifer pointed out. "Besides, Social Services will have their hands full with all those other relinquished babies. Which reminds me that I'd better get myself in gear." She had a big day ahead.

"You're going to be a terrific mother. For what it's worth, I wish…" Ian's words trailed off.

Jennifer felt the space between them thrum with longing. Then she saw that he'd missed shaving that same spot on his jaw. "Silly man," she murmured, and stroked her finger over it lightly. "You did it again."

His mouth closed the distance to hers. Brushed her lips and pulled away. "What I started to say was, I wish I could do more."

"You've done enough." *Or as much as you can.* "Good luck with that promotion."

Tony appeared in the doorway. "I talked to Miss Baron. You and I should discuss a few details before the social worker shows up, Jennifer."

"Of course."

"Look after her," Ian instructed the man. And out he went with his long, cocky stride.

Out of sight, out of the hospital and, while Jennifer might run into him a few more times before this baby story died down, most likely out of her life.

Chapter Twelve

"What kind of bush is this? I'd hate to end up with a rash," Pierre muttered.

"I think it's an azalea." Ian had waited in far worse circumstances to conduct interviews or, in this case, an ambush. "Perfectly safe."

"Yeah? Well, what's this ground cover? I wouldn't put it past this damn club to plant poison ivy all over their bloody exclusive premises," the cameraman grumbled. "My knees were sore, but I'm almost sorry I plopped on my butt. It's starting to itch."

"Doesn't do much for my dignity, either," Ian agreed. All the same, he felt justified crouching in wait for Judge Brandon Wycliff beside the parking lot of the man's country club.

Since the story containing Mrs. Wycliff's accusations broke on Sunday, the man had refused to return Ian's phone calls or speak to any members of the press. You could hardly blame him, considering that he faced serious criminal charges along with the scorn of the media. Late-night comedians were making hay out of the guy's escapades, and there'd been public outrage at the way he'd allegedly allowed a porno producer to approach his underage daughter.

He'd betrayed the public's trust by taking bribes, but to Ian the betrayal of his family's trust was even worse. The man ought to apologize publicly to his wife and child. Surely some kind of heart had to beat underneath that glib exterior.

Or maybe not. Sociopaths came in many guises. Some lurked in dark alleys or rode with gangs; some rose to political power; and others wore expensive suits and presided over courts.

Mrs. Wycliff had said the judge worked out regularly at his club. Sure enough, he'd arrived right on time this Thursday morning. A guard had stopped the news van at the entrance, so the two men had parked nearby, waited a while, then sneaked back on foot.

That was three hours ago, but his car, an overpriced luxury model, remained in its space. The judge must have finished working out and stayed for a late breakfast or early lunch.

Despite Ian's attempts to stretch and move around, his entire body had stiffened. What a ridiculous activity for two grown men, skulking in the bushes for hours. Yet he needed this interview. The story demanded a response, and Viktor and Flash News/Global's subscribers expected Ian to bring it.

He'd heard rumors that a woman who covered the Washington beat and an older man known for his science reporting were also being considered for the promotion. Both had clear fields of expertise, unlike Ian. Being a generalist might work against him, which meant he'd better prove to be such an outstanding generalist that he eclipsed his competitors.

Meanwhile, his grumbling stomach reminded him that he hadn't eaten since breakfast. Going without food didn't used to bother him. Was he getting soft—or just getting older?

"Here he comes." Pierre pointed toward a man with gray-tinged hair emerging from the building about thirty feet away. In his sky-blue designer suit, Judge Wycliff strutted as if he felt invulnerable. Behind him lurked a muscular fellow—the bodyguard, no doubt.

"Wait till they're well clear of the building." Luckily, they'd had to park some distance away. Ian didn't want them ducking for cover.

Pierre removed his lens cap. Ian activated the recorder in his pocket.

With a cautionary gesture, the bodyguard moved ahead of the judge toward the car. Apparently, the man's job included not only chauffeur duties but also starting the engine in case of a car bomb. Considering some of the criminals he'd associated with, the judge must have good reason to be afraid.

Ian almost felt sorry for him. Then he remembered the open-faced seventeen-year-old daughter whose own father had put her innocence at risk.

"Now!" Pierre sprang up and both men ran forward. Off to their right, the bodyguard bolted from the car. Ian waved a press card at him to forestall a physical attack. Not that the guy wouldn't still try to oust them, but he might take it easy on the roughhousing.

"Flash News/Global!" Ian shouted at the judge, who went rigid. Nowhere to hide, unless he dodged behind one of the parked vehicles, and how would that look on video? "I'm Ian Martin." He halted close enough to see the dark circles beneath his target's eyes. "I interviewed your ex-wife last weekend."

"I ought to sue you," the judge growled. "Now, beat it." Off to one side, the bodyguard hovered, as if uncertain how forcefully to intervene.

"I should think you'd seize this chance to apologize to your daughter publicly." Ian angled around, blocking the judge's escape.

Still, Wycliff could freeze him out. A simple "No comment," and he'd be off the hook.

However, the reference to his daughter appeared to rile the judge. "Libby knows I would never do anything to harm her."

"So you're saying this adult movie producer didn't offer her a job?" Ian prodded.

Wycliff licked his lips. In the bright sunlight, his complexion had a gray tinge. "My daughter is an aspiring actress. And a talented one."

"So you *approve* of her being solicited for a dirty movie?"

Pierre shifted the camera back and forth between the two of them. Capturing the whole business.

"Of course not!" Beads of sweat appeared on the judge's forehead. "The man's a friend of mine. Or used to be. He's a legitimate film producer, as well as—that other stuff. I had no idea he would do something like this."

Ian took no pleasure in his subject's discomfort, but the situation outraged him. "You're confirming your wife's account, then? You allowed your underage daughter to be approached about appearing in a sexually explicit film?"

"I didn't allow it!" Wycliff burst out. "My daughter was spending the weekend at my new home. I hosted a party, and while I was busy out by the pool with some friends, this lowlife made a…proposition. She got upset and called her mother to pick her up. That's all that happened."

What an infuriating scenario. The worst part was that the judge seemed to think he'd done nothing wrong.

"I've heard what kind of parties you like to throw," Ian fumed. "What exactly were you doing by the pool, Your Honor? Fooling around? Is that what you consider demonstrating appropriate fatherly behavior?"

Under the midday sun, sweat ran down Wycliff's face. "I was making sure my guests had a good time. That's all. A man is entitled to relax in his own home. There's nothing inappropriate about that. I've never done anything to harm my daughter. Not while I was married, and not since the divorce. Never!"

An unfamiliar fury churned inside Ian. "Oh, really? What about the way you cheated on your wife? What kind of message did that send to your daughter? It's a father's job to protect his family, not treat them like disposable toys. And what about those young women you paid to entertain you? They're somebody's daughters. Ever think maybe they had fathers like you, who taught them that men don't have to respect women?"

Wycliff's jaw clamped shut, and Ian could see him struggling to gain control. Raggedly, he muttered, "I've already said more than I should. Now, get out of my way."

When the man stumped forward, Ian stepped aside. No sense in risking physical contact, and besides, he had more than enough material for a story.

The guard must have put out an alert, because Ian

spotted two uniformed security men heading their way. Pierre, absorbed in filming the judge's retreat to his car, didn't notice until Ian tapped his shoulder.

"Oh, crap," said the cameraman, and they both took off for the bushes, behind which lay a break in the surrounding fence.

Whether because of their head start or because Security wasn't eager for a confrontation, they got away. Once they were in the van and Ian had a moment to reflect, he said, "Did Wycliff look like he might feel sick?"

"He ought to! That was some speech you gave." Behind the wheel, Pierre let out a whoop. "What got into you?"

"Did I go too far?" Ian hadn't meant to lose his temper.

"I figure you spoke for every outraged Joe Six-Pack in America," Pierre responded. "They'll eat it up."

"I'm not the story. Judge Wycliff is."

"You were part of the story today."

He'd been picturing Jennifer and Rosalie, Ian realized. Putting them in the roles of wife and daughter.

Well, whatever had sparked his outburst, it had pushed Wycliff into responding. Ian felt certain he'd recorded enough comments to fill out a written story as well as the video.

He wished he had the column already, so he could work in more of his own opinions. But for now, this would have to do.

ON SATURDAY AFTERNOON, by the time Jennifer and the baby joined Samantha and Lori, her friends had been busy for more than an hour at a strip mall filled with wedding shops. She'd begged their understanding, since

Rosalie could hardly be expected to keep quiet during a lengthy shopping expedition.

"Of course we understand!" Lori said as they sat around a low table, flipping through catalogs in a florist's shop. "Heck, at least you're *here,* which is more than I can say for my matron of honor."

Esther had stayed over in Washington for an extra week. According to Lori, her old friend had apparently made arrangements for some mysterious meetings she hadn't discussed in advance with anyone, including her husband. No wonder Tony had been uncharacteristically grumpy the past few days.

"You don't suppose she's having an affair, do you?" Samantha asked as she handed Jennifer a sample of the silver-and-blue invitations they'd selected earlier.

"No way!" Lori retorted. "Let's talk about something else."

Jennifer examined the invitation, which involved an incredible number of envelopes and inserts. "I can't believe how complicated this whole wedding business is."

"Oh, I love it!" In the catalog spread before them, Lori indicated a glorious bouquet, along with smaller, coordinated arrangements for bridesmaids. "This is cool, don't you think?"

"Absolutely," Jennifer agreed.

"Anyway, a wedding may be complicated, but it doesn't compare to adopting a baby."

She had to smile. "They're hardly the same thing."

"It's been a whole week," Samantha observed. "Any second thoughts?"

"Not a one. But I'll be glad when I'm done with the red tape." Making long-term plans to keep Rosalie had involved details from figuring out how to add the baby to her medical insurance to finding an adoption lawyer, since Jennifer couldn't expect Tony to handle all that.

Thank goodness for the baby equipment, which Ian had told her to keep. He'd e-mailed a couple of times and phoned on Wednesday to make sure she and Rosalie were doing well, but they hadn't discussed anything personal.

Not that she had expected to. Whatever they'd shared would always remain a treasured moment and nothing more, no matter how often she awoke missing him or caught herself longing for a glimpse of his endearing smile.

She felt fortunate to have her friends, who'd stopped by frequently to offer support and give her a break while she ran errands. Samantha truly didn't seem to harbor any ill feelings about being questioned. She'd said she was just glad they'd found the leak, and that Mark had agreed to let Judi continue volunteering.

"Motherhood is tough. I'd pick organizing a wedding any day." Lori jotted down the number identifying the flower arrangement. Then, leaning over the carriage, she crooned to Rosalie, "Yes, you are adorable, and it's fun to babysit you, but then I get to go home and play with Jared, and that's even more fun."

"But you *like* babies," Samantha pointed out.

"In small doses."

The pediatrician hesitated, but not for long. "Have you noticed that Jared likes babies, too? Sometimes he comes around the nursery and just watches them."

"He's a neonatologist," Lori countered. "Of course he loves babies! But he doesn't want one. He wants *me*."

"He's kind of young," Jennifer ventured. "You don't supposed in a few years he might change his mind?"

Instead of giving a direct answer, Lori riffled through the remaining pages in the catalog, scarcely glancing at the pictures. "Speaking of changing one's mind, Esther doesn't seem very interested in making preparations for *her* kid. All she talked about on the phone was Washington this and Washington that."

"Whatever she's up to, that little boy needs parents, and I feel kind of responsible," Samantha admitted.

"Why on earth?" Jennifer asked.

"The surrogate mother is my hairdresser. I'm the one who connected them, in a way."

Lori shut the catalog. "I can't ethically join this discussion because the surrogate is Dr. Rayburn's patient. Except to say that I really like her."

"Still, it's the Francos' baby, right?" Jennifer said. "Once she gives birth, she'll be out of the picture."

Lori and Samantha exchanged glances. "It's *his* baby," the pediatrician said. "Esther wasn't able to pro duce an egg."

"You mean it's the surrogate's genetic child?" Jennifer said. "How could she give it up?"

"Kate liked the idea of helping an infertile couple," Samantha replied. "She'd heard of another mom doing this and asked me about it, since I'm a doctor. I mentioned her to Tony."

"Helping people is one thing, but having a baby for total strangers?" Jennifer couldn't imagine doing that.

"It's not just altruism. She's a widow with a young son, and the Francos are paying a substantial amount. She mentioned wanting to establish a college fund."

"Now, there's one more thing I won't have to worry about, since I'm not going to have kids." The bride signaled to a clerk.

"What's next on the agenda?" Jennifer asked.

"After I order the flowers, I want to check out a photographer."

"Maybe I'll schedule a portrait of Rosalie while we're there," Jennifer said. "Ian sent me some nice candid shots, but I'd like a picture suitable for framing."

Samantha collected her purse. "I hope you guys will excuse me, but I have to bow out. That teen group I talked to begged me to come back. The girls have a lot of issues to discuss."

"What you're doing is wonderful," Jennifer added.

"It's a drop in the bucket. Well, see you later!"

A short time later, at the studio, Jennifer set an appointment for early the next afternoon. Then, while her friend met with the photographer, she pushed the baby carriage around the lobby, wistfully eyeing the glowing portraits of newlyweds, babies, recent graduates and families.

How handsome the fathers looked, dressed in dark suits, their sturdy presence anchoring the photos. When she was little, Jennifer used to long for a family like one of these with a real dad, not just Mimi's latest squeeze. If she'd had a father to turn to, she doubted she'd have fallen for Frank. Her brother, Bob, might have gone to college instead of drifting through high school with barely passing grades, although he seemed to be finding himself in the army.

How ironic that Ian didn't see himself fitting into one of these portraits. Jennifer's chest tightened. She'd almost phoned him yesterday after someone at work pointed out the video of him challenging that oily judge. *"It's a father's job to protect his family."*

He hadn't merely been reciting a line to get a reaction. He'd lashed out in true outrage, blue eyes burning with passion, light hair flying in the breeze. Half the women on the planet had probably fallen in love with him.

Jennifer swallowed a lump in her throat. *She* wasn't in love, but she'd skirted dangerously close. In any case, she was proud of Ian. It wasn't often that men like Judge Wycliff who abused their position got called to account bluntly and publicly.

Lori joined her, carrying a sheaf of paperwork. "Thank goodness we got a lot done today," the bride enthused. "Next weekend, once Esther gets back, we can decide on the cake and the rest of the menu."

"Sounds good to me."

At her car, Jennifer strapped Rosalie in the safety seat and folded the stroller away. "I'm glad I've got you," she told the baby fiercely. "I'll never let you down. I promise."

The infant watched her intently, love evident in every sweet curve of her face and wriggle of her tiny body. What a precious gift.

Behind the wheel, Jennifer switched on the radio, tuned to an all-news station. Keeping abreast of events that might unexpectedly affect the hospital was part of her job.

After a commercial, the announcer's deep voice proclaimed, "A spokesman at UCLA Medical Center says Judge Brandon Wycliff died today of a massive heart attack. The judge, who faced corruption charges for allegedly taking bribes, collapsed at his home during the night and was found this morning by a housekeeper."

A chill ran through Jennifer. Despite her low opinion of the man, it bothered her that he'd died alone.

After pulling into her carport, she extracted Rosalie and wheeled her along a walkway toward their building. She scarcely noticed a blur of movement from a lounge chair in the common area until a man rushed toward her.

Her pulse rocketed. Almost at the same moment, to her relief, she recognized Ian. Far from the glamorous figure in the video, he had a coffee stain on his shirt and a strained redness to his eyes.

"Are you all right?" she asked.

"No." He shoved both hands in his pockets. "No, I'm not sure I am."

Jennifer hated seeing him so distressed. Yet she was glad that, when he needed someone to turn to, he'd chosen her.

No matter where it led.

Chapter Thirteen

A call from the night editor at Flash News/Global had awakened Ian around 6:00 a.m. A local wire service that kept tabs on law enforcement and other emergency services was reporting Judge Wycliff's death from a coronary.

Ian's first thought had been, *Why didn't I tell him to see a doctor?*

Because he wasn't the man's keeper, he'd reminded himself. Then he'd flown into action, racing to the bureau, leaving a message for Mrs. Wycliff requesting her reaction, and pushing until he managed to reach someone in the federal prosecutor's office, who insisted the investigation would continue, focusing on those suspected of attempting to buy justice.

Eventually a spokeswoman had returned his call to read a statement saying that Mrs. Wycliff and her daughter wished to mourn privately. Funeral arrangements would be private.

Ian couldn't stop thinking about the daughter. Despite Wycliff's faults, he'd deserved a chance to reconcile with her, to apologize. If not for his own sake, then for hers.

Maybe if Ian hadn't pressed so hard, he'd have lived long enough to get the chance.

You aren't God. You don't cause people to suffer heart failure. But he hadn't done anything to help the man, either.

At his editor's request, Ian had driven to the courthouse and stood in front to record a video segment about the judge's demise. Then he'd returned to the bureau to update the written story as new information came in.

Through it all, a hard knot had formed in Ian's gut. Coffee couldn't wash it away, and hard work failed to dissolve it. He had to find a place where the people around him weren't celebrating the story as if he'd scored some kind of coup. He had to talk to someone who might understand that a man's death was a tragedy, no matter how unworthy a life he'd led.

Finally he'd signed out and driven to Safe Harbor. He supposed he should have called ahead, but he hadn't wanted to risk a polite refusal. When he discovered that Jennifer was out, he'd simply tried her at her condo. She wasn't at home, so he tumbled into the nearest lounge chair and waited.

Now that she'd finally arrived, the concern on her face nearly unraveled him. "Can we talk?" he choked out.

"Sure." She didn't ask what this was about. Maybe she'd already guessed.

Inside the condo, she settled on the couch. Ian remained on his feet, unable to stop pacing.

Hard to realize that little more than a week had passed since he'd first set foot in this place. It seemed so familiar now, as did the beautiful woman holding the baby in the crook of her arm. Ian felt as if months had passed—and as if he'd been away far too long.

"I'm sorry," he blurted.

"For what?" As she adjusted the bottle for Rosalie, Jennifer radiated serenity.

The sight of them steadied him. "For barging in without calling. I needed to be around someone normal. Someone decent who doesn't think having a judge drop dead is a terrific media event."

"I feel bad for his family," she said. "Especially his daughter."

"I met her, just for a minute. She seemed so vulnerable." Ian ran his fingers roughly through his hair, not caring how randomly it sprang back. "I could see he wasn't well, but I kept grilling him. That's the way you have to act in an ambush interview. Strike hard and startle them into saying something quotable." He heard the scorn cutting through his words, scorn at his own behavior.

"You think your aggression caused his heart attack? Ian, that's impossible," Jennifer chided.

He tried to figure out why this bothered him so much. "I lost my objectivity," he admitted. "I stopped being a reporter and became an advocate. Who the hell do I think I am? The person who deserved an advocate was Libby, and what did I do? Took away her father."

"Stop," Jennifer said.

He was being unfair in unloading on her. "I apologize, again. This isn't your problem."

Starting to lean forward, she accidentally jostled the baby, who let out a squeak of protest. Putting Rosalie to her shoulder, Jennifer patted the little one's back. "I meant, stop beating up on yourself, Ian. You were magnificent."

He stared at her blankly. "Magnificent at what?"

"On the video. You did a great job. He deserved to be confronted with the hard questions."

"Those weren't questions, it was a speech. Hardly the stuff of fair reporting." Restlessly, he cut a trail around the carpet.

"What's with you?" Jennifer asked quietly. "You don't sound like the same man who stepped all over my toes the night we met."

"Excuse me?"

"That interview in the hallway. You kept prodding me on my sore point, about whether I wanted a baby. All you cared about was making an impact on video."

He recalled how determined he'd been to find a story, no matter what. Still, he hadn't been *that* big a jerk. "Public relations is your job. You were fair game."

"And Judge Wycliff wasn't?"

Ian had to concede the point. "Well, sure."

Jennifer resumed feeding the baby. "Why do you feel responsible for his daughter?"

The query startled him. "I guess it comes from being around Rosalie. She's so helpless."

"No more than any other infant."

"That's the point. Adults have an obligation to protect kids. All kids, and especially the ones who depend on them."

Ian stopped pacing to study the tiny girl. He'd never worried about his nieces, probably because they were so far off and seemed secure. But he'd seen Sunny hand over Rosalie and heard the story of her uncaring, self-centered father. At a gut level, he felt as if she'd been entrusted to Jennifer and, in some ways, to him.

Why the hell am I thinking that?

"Here." Jennifer tossed him a small blanket. "Put that on your shoulder."

There was barely time to comply before she transferred the baby into his arms. Incredibly small, fragrant with baby powder and yet solid, Rosalie nestled against him with a contented sigh. "I think she recognizes me."

"You've been around her a lot. Samantha says babies recognize their mothers' odor, so why not yours?"

Ian winced. "I hate to think how I smell after a day at the bureau. Stale coffee, stress and old cigarette smoke." That particular stench had seeped so deeply into the furniture that it lingered even though workplace smoking had been banned in California for years.

"She can tell it's you under there," Jennifer murmured. "Anyway, there's nothing like holding a baby to reconnect you to what matters in life."

What matters in life. Like becoming a father, as Viktor had. Suddenly, it struck Ian that he wanted that, too. Not right away, but someday. "I've heard of maternal instincts, but I didn't know it happened to men."

"Guess you were wrong."

On the other hand, he didn't mean to give the impression that he was about to chuck his dreams for some desk job. Concerned, he studied Jennifer's face for any sign that she was making assumptions. Years ago, he'd dated a woman for a few months in London, when he was twenty-five and barely mature enough to keep track of his laundry. One day, she'd begun insisting they could save money by moving in together. After a new assignment came through, he was embarrassed to recall, he'd broken up with her by phone and caught the next plane out of England.

Now, however, Ian detected nothing more than amusement in Jennifer's expression. For reasons he'd rather not think about, that gave him a twinge of disappointment.

"Tired?" she asked, apparently mistaking his silence for weariness.

"No. Just restless."

"You could use a minivacation."

"What did you have in mind?"

"Nothing beats lying on the sand listening to the waves." She slanted him a grin. "Now that school's back in session, we should be able to find a parking space."

"You, my lady, are a genius."

"Not even close."

"I beg to differ. I'll bet you look brilliant in a bikini."

"Let's find out."

It wasn't only holding a baby that reconnected a man to what mattered, Ian reflected as he handed over Rosalie and went to fetch the swim trunks from his duffel bag. It was also being around a woman who understood what he needed even before he did.

Scary. But exhilarating, too.

JENNIFER DID HER BEST to fix that afternoon in her mind. The sparkle of sun on water as Ian cut through the waves, swimming out until she lost sight of him against the horizon, and then stroking his way back. The brightness in Rosalie's cheeks as, protected by a beach umbrella, the well-wrapped baby lolled on an oversize towel. The tangy flavor of fried clams dipped in chili sauce, bought from a nearby seafood shop.

And later, the grit of sand beneath their feet as she and Ian showered together, and the slow build of passion as their water-slicked bodies came together. The sodden tangle of towels tossed aside, the rush to her bed, the longed-for coupling that drove out everything else in a burst of pure joy.

Afterward, curled against Ian, Jennifer was grateful that he'd come to her when he needed comfort. Was it really impossible to have a relationship with a man who spent most of his life on the road? They might never have more than moments like these, but wasn't that better than nothing? She'd long ago recognized that the kind of man she craved would never, in the long run, turn out to be the kind of man she could lean on.

She'd have to be careful how she broached the subject, though. If only he felt the same way.

On Sunday morning, breakfast had become an almost familiar ritual, not taken for granted, yet comfortable. "We might even use up some of these jams and jellies," she commented as they lingered over coffee.

"I could bring you more—" He broke off.

From his travels. Jennifer fought her impulse to seize on the unspoken offer. He'd bitten it back, after all. "Well, if you happen to get to L.A. again, that would be great."

"I don't get here often." He was withdrawing. Not only through his words, but he'd averted his gaze to the window, as if her patio held something of great interest.

"I suppose not."

Then he fixed on her again, the azure of his eyes vivid in the morning light. "If I do, though, would it be all right if I call you?"

"Of course." Her heart leaped. *Don't ask for too much.* "I'll be curious to find out if Rosalie remembers you that long."

"You could e-mail photos."

That seemed safe enough. "I'd be glad to."

He dug into his wallet and handed her a card with his e-mail address. "You know, last time we had a conversation like this, I found out you were holding back."

Jennifer wasn't sure what he meant. "About what?"

"The surrendered babies. Any more secrets I should know about? I just don't want to look like an idiot in case...never mind. I don't even know why I brought it up."

She took a deep breath. "Do I have secrets? Sure. Dark and deep. But I'll save them for my memoirs, if I ever write any."

He regarded her quizzically, as if unsure how seriously to take her. Then he shrugged. "It's not as if I'm entitled to the whole truth and nothing but."

Jennifer checked her watch. "Speaking of photos, Rosalie and I have an appointment at a studio in a little over an hour."

"You don't mess around. She's only been with you a week and you've got the whole formal thing lined up."

"If I seem organized, I assure you, it's an illusion." Jennifer rose, her mind filling with all the things she had to do to get ready. "Having a baby to raise means taking everything day by day."

"But you're happy?" Ian asked.

Suddenly she realized she was. Even though it all felt a bit tentative and fragile, she was happier than she could ever recall.

"I am," Jennifer said. *And if I can see you again before you leave L.A., I'll be even happier.* But she decided it would be wiser not to say that.

Besides, it was enough for right now that they

worked side by side clearing the dishes and putting away the food. Moving in synch, at ease with each other and with the silence.

As if they belonged together. And for this brief span of time, they did.

ON THE DRIVE BACK TO L.A., the radio had nothing new to say about the judge. Luckily, there'd been no major developments while Ian was lolling on the beach and spending a memorable night with Jennifer.

He recognized what this meant. With his main story basically finished, there was no reason for him to stick around L.A. Sure, the rock singer and the actress would no doubt keep throwing brickbats at each other as their all-too-public divorce battle dragged on, but the local staff could handle that.

Usually by this point in the wrap-up, Ian became impatient for the next challenge. Eager to be surrounded by the scents and colors of another culture, by the sound of a foreign language.

Still, he wished he could spend a few more days at the beach, a few more mornings breakfasting with Jennifer and the baby. How long before he came this way again? Would Rosalie be walking already? Would Jennifer welcome him with the same gentle acceptance he'd found today?

Amazingly, she'd managed to diminish Ian's guilt over failing to protect Libby Wycliff from the loss of her father. Now that the initial shock had faded, he supposed he'd been egotistical to imagine that he'd had the power to prevent the judge's death.

As he transitioned to another freeway, Ian became

keenly aware of the distance lengthening between him and Safe Harbor. It seemed unlikely he'd ever find out what supposedly deep, dark secrets Jennifer had referred to. While she might have been joking about that, he didn't think so.

He wished she'd trusted him enough to confide in him. But he couldn't blame her for not baring her soul to a man who was about to leave.

Whatever she hadn't told him, it was none of his business.

Chapter Fourteen

Jennifer began the week, as usual, by reviewing supervisors' summaries of weekend events for anything that might be newsworthy, for good or ill. Fortunately, things had been quiet: no more surrendered babies and no further incursions by the news media.

The coast appeared clear for her to start on the monthly mailer, a mixture of health tips and medical news that the hospital sent to the community. "We'll have to address the baby issue," Jennifer observed while reviewing ideas in Willa's small office next to hers.

"I wrote a poem to thank the mothers for bringing them here." The assistant handed it to her. "It's kind of sentimental, but don't you think it captures the spirit? We could frame this with cute little cupids. That way we don't actually show the babies and breach their privacy."

Jennifer scanned the poem. "Well done. Great idea." The community enjoyed this kind of approach, judging by the positive response to a holiday tribute Willa had written to the nurses who worked while others celebrated. "You have a knack for going straight to the heart."

Her assistant sighed. "Tell that to my kids. They stopped sharing their feelings with me in junior high."

"They're teenagers. They'll appreciate you when they're older." On the far side of the administrative suite, a door slammed. "I wonder what that's about."

"I don't know, but Tony marched in here this morning looking ready to punch someone, and disappeared into Mark's office."

Jennifer hadn't heard of any bone of contention between the attorney and the administrator, so it must be something else. "What do you suppose— Never mind." She dragged her thoughts back to the mailer. "Let's go with this. It's lovely."

Later that morning, she nearly bumped into Tony as he exited his office. "Can I help with anything?" Jennifer asked.

He scowled. "Yeah, you can buy me a straitjacket and throw me in a padded cell." And out he stalked.

What on earth?

After tapping on Mark's door, Jennifer peered inside. "What's going on with Tony?"

The administrator regarded her grimly. "It's a personal matter."

She waited for him to elaborate. The moment lengthened. Okay, she could take a hint. "Sorry to intrude."

Stepping out, Jennifer decided to see if Dr. Jared Sellers, Lori's fiancé, had time to fill her in on a cooling machine the hospital had acquired to treat newborns who'd suffered oxygen deprivation. She'd love to write about it for the mailer.

The easygoing neonatologist proved eager to show her the machine. "Let's say the umbilical cord chokes off the newborn's air supply, potentially causing brain damage," he said as she took notes. "By wrapping the baby's head in this tubing and circulating cold water, we can lower the infant's temperature slightly. Doing this for up to seventy-two hours reduces the risk of cerebral palsy or other disabilities, although it's by no means a cure-all."

She shivered, thinking of Rosalie. "Isn't it dangerous to chill a baby like that?"

He pointed to a heating element. "We pamper the rest of our little patients' bodies and monitor them constantly." Warming to his subject—she'd better not use *that* phrase in her story, Jennifer mused—Jared went on to explain that, while the technology might be new, therapeutic cooling dated back to the days of Hippocrates, the ancient Greek considered by some historians to be the first real physician. He had recommended that soldiers' wounds be packed in snow and ice.

After snapping pictures of Jared with the machine, Jennifer teased, "Do you plan to keep that mustache for the wedding?"

He fingered the thin line on his upper lip. "That's up to my bride. She's calling the shots." Jared's smile faded. "Although she's a little freaked out this morning."

"About what?"

"Where we'll hold the reception. But I'm sure she'll figure something out." His beeper sounded. "Duty calls." Before she could quiz him further, he strode away.

The reception had been planned for Tony and Esther's house. There was obviously a connection between the attorney's bad mood and Lori's concern, but what?

Since it was almost noon, Jennifer went by the day-care center to check on Rosalie. Although disappointed to find the infant sound asleep, she was glad her daughter had apparently adapted to the new environment. According to the supervisor, the baby had seemed entertained watching the other children play and had taken her bottles right on schedule.

Reassured, Jennifer headed to the cafeteria to meet her friends. After choosing a salad, she spotted Lori in a sunny corner of the outdoor patio, poking furiously at her pasta. In the sunshine, her freckles stood out like angry red dots. If Jennifer hadn't known better, she'd fear her friend was coming down with a rash.

Jennifer set her tray on the table. "You look upset."

"You might say that." Lori stabbed the food in front of her, which she'd reduced to a mash of broccoli bits, carrots and noodles. It appeared to have been today's special, pasta primavera.

Samantha joined them, carrying a large sandwich and a carton of milk. Straightforward as always, she plopped down and announced, "I've been hearing rumors about the Francos all morning, but none of them make any sense. What gives?"

"If there's any problem with the wedding plans, you know we'll help," Jennifer added.

Lori glowered at them. "I am not some Bridezilla who thinks this whole thing is about me."

"We would never think that," Samantha assured her. "Now spill."

"My best friend, the girl who used to practically live at my house because her rich parents were always flying off on trips and she couldn't stand being alone, the woman who insisted that my wedding colors coordinate with *her* decor…" Lori broke off to take a deep swig of mineral water.

"In other words, Esther," Jennifer filled in.

"Yeah, her, although I'm not sure I'll ever be able to speak her name again."

"She got back from Washington yesterday, right?" Samantha prompted.

"And I called her all happy and eager to talk about our much-delayed shopping trip," Lori grumbled. "You know what she said?"

They didn't.

"She said, 'Don't count on me.' Can you believe that? She didn't even have the courtesy or the nerve to say that she won't be part of my wedding, just 'Don't count on me.' Like I'd invited her to a cocktail party!"

"Why can't you count on her?" Jennifer hoped they were about to unlock this morning's mystery.

"She's accepted a job in the U.S. Attorney General's office, in Washington, D.C. Starting immediately. She boasted about what a great career move it is and how everyone should be thrilled for her," Lori fumed.

"No wonder Tony was out of sorts." Jennifer wondered how his wife had persuaded him to agree to this huge step. "A move like that is a big deal. She's got a new job, but what about him?"

"I'm not sure Tony's going with her." In response to their startled glances, Lori explained, "She didn't tell him what she was doing. Completely blindsided him."

"How could she do that?" Jennifer spluttered.

"She went on and on about what a huge break this is

and how she couldn't bear to give it up, so she didn't bother asking."

"What about their baby?" Samantha demanded. "Is she giving him up, too?"

"I got that impression."

"How could she?" Jennifer had to struggle to keep her voice low. "I thought she was the one who wanted a baby in the first place."

"Probably because she learned she was infertile," Samantha growled. "That woman can't bear to hear the word no."

"She's always been spoiled," Lori conceded. "And selfish. But I never imagined she'd go this far."

How could a person simply toss her family aside? Jennifer wondered. Well, perhaps they were being unfair to Esther. She might still work things out with Tony.

For once, though, Lori seemed in no mood for further conversation.

AFTER SENDING HIS EDITOR a follow-up story filled with quotes from former colleagues who regretted the downfall of Judge Wycliff's once-promising legal mind, Ian forced himself to do the task he dreaded.

He dialed Eleanor Wycliff's number again. Not her personal line, which she hadn't revealed, but the one that rang through to her home office. While she might still refuse to speak to him, he had to try.

A spokeswoman answered. Instead of giving Ian short shrift, she said, "I believe Mrs. Wycliff would like to speak to you."

Oh, great. Although as a reporter he was obligated

to keep trying to contact her, he didn't look forward to being hauled over the coals. Despite the woman's aversion to her slimy ex-husband, death had a way of bringing out hidden feelings.

She came on the line. "Mr. Martin?" He would have recognized that patrician voice anywhere.

"Mrs. Wycliff, I hope Libby's all right." He braced for whatever came next.

"Thanks to you, my daughter's fine."

"Thanks to me?" He didn't detect any sarcasm in her tone.

"On Friday, my ex-husband called to say he was sorry," she said. "Apparently, you suggested it."

Ian had, indeed. "I never expected him to listen."

"Well, he apologized first to me, for cheating and behaving so disrespectfully to me. Can you believe it? We were married for eighteen years and not once did he say he was sorry, about anything."

Ian pictured her shaking that head of silver hair in amazement. "I suppose you saw the video...."

"Yes, and your words obviously got through to him." Eleanor cleared her throat. "Then he talked to our daughter. I didn't hear what they discussed, but afterward, she was crying. The good kind of crying. She said, 'He really does love me.' I think she'd begun to doubt it."

Ian's throat tightened. "I'm glad he did that."

"The next day, he died," Eleanor continued, a touch of amazement in her voice. "If it weren't for you, he'd have gone to his grave without making amends. We owe you a great deal, Mr. Martin."

Gravity seemed to lighten for Ian, as if he'd been

rescued from trudging across the planet Jupiter. "I was afraid our interview might have contributed to his heart attack."

"I don't see how. Reconciling with Libby should have been good for his heart," she responded. "You gave him peace, and you gave us closure."

"I appreciate your telling me this."

"You can quote me if you want," she added. "But I'd rather you didn't."

"I think it's best that we keep this private."

After the call ended, Ian sat staring at his computer screen, scarcely noticing the din of phones and conversation in the newsroom. What a sense of elation.

"Hey, Martin!" yelled the day supervisor. "Somebody here to see you."

"Who?"

"Didn't give a name."

Hardly anyone ventured into the Flash News/Global offices except the occasional publicist, outraged story subject or nut job. Warily, Ian went to the receptionist's desk.

He didn't recognize either of the two people standing there, both clearly nervous as they watched him approach. The woman, in her early forties, leaned on a cane, while the man beside her stood crookedly, one shoulder lower than the other. They must have suffered serious injuries, he surmised.

Ian introduced himself.

"We know who you are, Mr. Martin. We've seen you on the Internet," said the man. "I'm John McCoy and this is my wife, Andrea."

"What can I do for you?" he asked.

"You can write the truth about Jennifer Serra." Bitterness laced the man's words. "She's the criminal who did this to us, and she's never paid for it. We're here to see that she does."

Chapter Fifteen

After lunch, Jennifer set to work on the article about the cooling machine. Pieces for the mailer had to be short and upbeat, and this one suited the formula perfectly.

She was halfway through when her peripheral vision caught someone standing in the office doorway. At first glance she imagined it might be Ian—obviously wishful thinking—and then, with a spurt of pleasure, she saw that it really was him.

But the tightness in his jaw told her this wasn't a social visit. "What's wrong?" she asked.

"We need to talk."

As she got to her feet, Jennifer found it hard to breathe. What could have happened to bring him here in the middle of the day? "Ian, is your family all right?"

He blinked in surprise. "Yes, of course."

"Well?"

She missed the sparkle in his gaze and his usual easy stance. He'd gone very stiff, very controlled. "I had a visit from two people who claim to know you from the past. John and Andrea McCoy."

The blood rushed out of her head, leaving a

dizzying void. A hand on the desk steadied her, but only marginally.

This was what she'd feared from the moment she'd allowed herself to be thrust into the public's attention on Ian's video. Now the ghosts of twelve years ago had returned.

She struggled to speak. "You're going to write about this? Ian, it's old news."

He folded his arms. "They're angry about all the publicity portraying you as a heroine. They said they've tried to put the past behind them, but seeing you in the news has raked up old, painful feelings. Mrs. McCoy's been having nightmares, and some of her family members insist that's because you never paid for what you did to them. If I don't write about this, they might go to someone else—someone far less sympathetic. Please tell me your side of the story."

He'd come here in person, willing to listen. That was a good thing, Jennifer told herself. But it didn't feel very good.

Apparently, the McCoys wanted revenge. In a sense, she didn't blame them. But life had taken its own revenge, long ago.

Behind Ian loomed Mark, a few inches taller and considerably bulkier than the journalist. "Is this reporter harassing you?" the administrator asked.

She appreciated her boss's protectiveness. But she wondered how long that would last once the truth came out.

"No. I have to explain something to him. Can I fill you in later?" To her embarrassment, Jennifer heard her voice quaver. She hoped Mark wouldn't insist on sitting in during their interview. It might be more than she could bear.

He didn't argue. "I'll trust your judgment."

When he was gone, Ian regarded her questioningly. "Where's a good place?"

"Not in the hospital." Too many ears, and besides, the walls were closing in today. "There's a park about a block away. How about that?"

He agreed. As they walked to the elevators, Jennifer did her best to assume a casual air for the sake of any onlookers.

But inside, she felt as if she were about to face a firing squad.

In the park, Ian found a bench far from the busy playground. Such a serene setting, with a light fall breeze rustling through palm trees and half a dozen small children calling to one another as they played beneath their mothers' watchful gazes.

Then he saw the pain etched on Jennifer's face. He'd never meant to bring anything like this down on top of her.

Reluctantly he took out his digital recorder. As he'd half expected, Jennifer waved it away.

"Just take notes, if you must," she said.

"Okay." He didn't plan to use audio, anyway, and he'd long ago developed his own form of shorthand.

"How are they?" she asked.

"Who?"

"The McCoys."

She appeared genuinely concerned. *If only they knew her, maybe they'd let go of their anger.* But how likely was that, given what they'd suffered?

"They were pretty badly injured." The shattered bones, torn ligaments and other injuries had left an indelible imprint on their bodies. "Mrs. McCoy spent years learning to walk again, and her husband still has problems with his left arm. He had to give up house painting, although he's landed a decent job managing an auto parts store."

Jennifer stared at a child running after an errant rubber ball. "I feel so awful about them."

"They said you were driving a getaway car. That you ran a red light and broadsided them." He couldn't reconcile the image of a criminally reckless teenager with the troubled woman before him, but they'd shown him a copy of the police report as well as old newspaper clippings.

"That's true, as far as it goes." Jennifer's fingers laced together in her lap. "You remember I told you about Frank, the guy I dated when I was seventeen?"

"They said he robbed a liquor store." Ian hadn't let on to the McCoys that he recognized the name. He'd seen no reason to confide any more about his friendship with Jennifer than they'd already surmised from the tone of his last article.

Her gaze grew faraway, as if she were peering back through time. "One night when he picked me up, he was acting strung out, jumpy. I knew he used drugs occasionally, but that's the first time it occurred to me that he was addicted. I asked him to take me home." A deep breath. "Instead, he stopped in front of a convenience store and told me to get behind the wheel."

Ian pictured a younger version of Jennifer, confused and apprehensive. "You had no idea what he was planning?"

She shook her head. "He said he was out of cigarettes. I was actually glad Frank let me drive, because I didn't think he was in any fit condition. Later I found out he was broke and in debt—the worst kind. He'd swiped drugs from a dealer he was staying with."

Across the park Ian caught curious glances from a couple of women sitting around a picnic table. He wondered if they recognized him or Jennifer, and was relieved that they made no attempt to approach.

She continued talking, caught up in her story now. "If he didn't pay for them fast, he'd have ended up in an alley, probably dead. The gun he used, he stole that from his roommate, too. He apparently had some fantasy about scoring a lot of money from the robbery, enough to repay the guy and take me to Mexico. Obviously he wasn't thinking straight."

"So you moved behind the wheel. What happened next?"

"He came running out with the clerk in pursuit. I thought at first he'd swiped a six-pack. When he jumped in the car, I told him I'd pay for it. Then I saw the gun."

"He aimed it at you?" The McCoys had doubted the threat was real. "You honestly believe he'd have shot you?"

"He wasn't rational," she insisted. "I had no idea what he'd do. He kept yelling at me to hit the gas, and I just obeyed on instinct."

"The cops picked up your trail." The clerk had hit a silent alarm, according to the police report, and a patrol car had responded from a mere block away.

"They got there fast." Jennifer shuddered. "I wanted to pull over. I knew we couldn't escape. But when Frank pressed that gun to my temple, I panicked."

"How fast were you going?"

"I'm still not sure. There were sirens screaming everywhere. It felt surreal. I just wanted it to end, so I stepped on the gas, harder than I intended. I didn't even see the red light. The car seemed to come out of nowhere. I jerked the wheel, but Frank fell against me, and I lost control. The next thing I knew, I was in the hospital."

He recalled her telling him about a crash, that morning a little more than a week ago when they'd first made love. "You were five months pregnant. You lost the baby."

She swallowed. "At the hospital I was numb. I couldn't take it in. My little boy was gone. A detective came in and told me about the couple I'd hit, that the woman was in critical condition. He kept emphasizing how even if she survived, she might never walk again. It was horrible."

"You agreed to testify against Frank in return for immunity?" The McCoys had been especially bitter about that part.

Tears glimmered in her eyes. "I think the detective was out for blood, but later, the district attorney determined they didn't have a case. I had no criminal record, there were no drugs or alcohol in my system and thank goodness the clerk had seen Frank point the gun at me. I'd have testified anyway. He deserved to go to prison."

"Is he still there?"

She nodded. "He got a long sentence. Turned out he'd had a prior conviction."

Another matter occurred to Ian. "What about your miscarriage? Frank could have been charged with causing your baby's death."

"With me driving? I doubt a jury would have gone

for that, and I guess the D.A drew the same conclusion." Her shoulders trembled. "Besides, I didn't want my personal grief splashed across the newspapers. I tried my best to keep it quiet."

"So the McCoys never knew about him?"

"Not as far as I know."

Perhaps it might have helped them understand that Jennifer hadn't escaped scot-free, after all. "I'd like to arrange a meeting between you and them. To give them all the facts. Maybe this can be a story about reconciliation instead of payback."

"I doubt they could ever forgive me, after what they've endured." Her forehead furrowed. "They had two children, didn't they? Thank goodness they weren't in the car. How are they?"

That had been the positive part of the interview. "Both doing well. Their daughter's a senior in high school with excellent grades, and their son's attending a private college on scholarship. They had to grow up fast, but they learned to take responsibility, their parents said."

The assurance didn't seem to cheer Jennifer. "They were robbed of their childhood. If you want me to meet with the McCoys, that's fine. Not to make excuses, but to apologize."

"May I tell them about the miscarriage?"

"That would sound like I'm trying to manipulate them into forgiving me. If we meet and it comes out, fine. But otherwise, no."

Ian understood her sense of guilt. He'd experienced that with Judge Wycliff, even though he hadn't caused the judge's death. Still, he wished he had something to offer the McCoys, who didn't strike him as inclined to extend the olive branch.

Well, he'd do his best. "I'll be right back," he said, and went to make the call.

DESPITE THE ACTIVITY surging around her—children running and calling to one another, moms sharing a laugh—Jennifer felt drained. Being forced to relive those agonizing events hadn't provided any release. Instead, it had stirred emotions she'd prefer to keep under wraps.

But while they might have been buried, they certainly hadn't died.

She tried to imagine what it would mean for her now that the McCoys insisted on going public. Under ordinary circumstances, such an old case probably wouldn't hold much interest for the public. But thanks to Ian—unintentionally, of course—Jennifer had become news again. People all over the world had read about her and Rosalie. She'd been cheered as a Good Samaritan, and now she was about to be revealed as practically a criminal.

The press loved stories like that. Tearing down idols. Not that she'd ever considered herself a role model for anyone.

The downcast expression on Ian's face as he returned revealed the bad news before he spoke. "They refused. The very idea stressed Mrs. McCoy. They even started threatening to go elsewhere with their story. It was quite a job calming them down."

The last, faint hope for avoiding catastrophe withered inside Jennifer. "I'd rather you wrote the article than anyone else. I'm sure you'll tell the story fairly."

He conceded the point. "At least let me give a complete picture. Jennifer, I want to put in the part about your miscarriage."

As a publicist, she realized that would paint her in a more positive light. But she didn't want this to become a battle between her and the McCoys for the public's sympathy. "They deserve their day in the sun. Coming forward must have been painful for them, and I refuse to make it harder than it needs to be."

"This could get nasty," Ian warned.

He didn't have to tell her that she might lose her job, her home, her friends…. Jennifer struggled to stay calm. *Take this one moment at a time.*

"What about the baby?" he said. "What if Sunny changes her mind?"

Her stomach constricted. She hadn't considered that. "I think she'll understand."

"So do I. As I mentioned, she told me she thought you'd been wounded, like her."

What an amazing young woman. "She called that one right. And now, if we're done, I'd better get back to work." Jennifer stood, only to discover her knees were almost too shaky to hold her.

Ian caught her arm. "I never meant to stir up this kind of trouble."

"I know. Besides, I always figured something like this would happen sooner or later." She shrugged weakly. "I hope it'll give the McCoys some comfort, at least."

He kept his hand on the small of her back, supporting her as they set out. "Here's a bit of positive news. Mrs. Wycliff called to say that the day before he died, the judge apologized to his daughter."

"Feel better?" she asked him.

"I did, until the McCoys showed up."

She longed to snuggle against him, to lean on his strength in more ways than one. But Jennifer had to stand on her own two feet, now and always. "Ian, don't worry about the impact on me. It's your job to write this story. I hope the publicity helps you get your promotion."

He groaned. "Don't even mention it."

"Why not?"

"I've always figured my work would make the world a better place. Now I'm not so sure."

"It'll work out." She tried to hold on to that thought as they reached the hospital parking lot and separated with a hug.

Despite his obvious regret, she could tell Ian's mind was racing ahead to his article. As for her, she'd promised to fill Mark in.

That meant dredging up the whole sorry tale all over again. But she intended to keep her obligations, no matter the cost.

Chapter Sixteen

The firestorm broke Monday night. Ian's story, with photos of the McCoys—they'd declined to appear on video—hit the Web around dinnertime and made the news nationwide.

He'd expected a big response, but nothing like the flood of phone calls and e-mails, or the swell of blogs and Web postings cited by Flash News/Global's monitoring service. And not only did hordes of reporters descend on the hospital, they also showed up at the McCoys' home.

"It never occurred to me that they'd come *here,*" Andrea McCoy told Ian on the phone. "What should I do?"

"What do you want to do?" He tilted his chair back onto two legs. Flash News/Global really ought to buy swivel chairs for its employees, considering the long hours they put in, he mused.

"Ignore them," she responded ruefully. "My husband tried talking to them, but they kept pushing him to say nasty things about Jennifer Serra. That she ought to be put in prison, or have her baby taken away. We never meant for this to become a vendetta. I suppose I really didn't think it through. My children were angry, and somehow I imagined that telling the truth would make things better. I certainly don't want to deprive her little baby of a home."

Ian considered proposing again that they meet with Jennifer, but decided to wait for the McCoys themselves to suggest it. "She won't lose Rosalie. The birth mother's sticking by her." He'd talked to Jennifer earlier and been pleased to hear of Sunny's support.

Her boss had stood by her also. But should this flood of negative publicity continue, she'd said, she wasn't sure how the hospital's corporate owners would react. If the stern Ms. Yashimoto was a fair representation of management, and he suspected so, that didn't bode well.

Nothing he could do about that. Unfortunately.

"You did a fine job with the article," Andrea was saying.

"Thanks."

"The thing is, even though you quoted us accurately, I don't like the way we came across."

That baffled him. "How do you mean?"

"We sounded bitter," she conceded.

"I'm sure the public understands." Ian righted his chair abruptly as a student intern rushed past, nearly toppling him. The girl waved an apology before hurrying on between neighboring desks.

She ought to go home at this ridiculous hour. Nearly eleven o'clock. And so should he, except that a solitary motel room hardly qualified as home.

Ian's thoughts flew to a certain cheerful kitchen, and upstairs to the baby's room, and down the hall to the bedroom filled with Jennifer's essence even when she wasn't there. But she would be there, surely, at this hour.

He shook away the thought. That was all the press needed, to spot him sneaking into Jennifer's condo in the middle of the night. Not that she'd mentioned any reporters showing up at her address, but it might happen. And that would reflect badly on them both.

If only I didn't miss her so damn much.

"I guess most people sympathize with us," Andrea muttered. "But I got a phone call earlier from a woman I know from church. She said I should let go of my anger, for my soul's sake. How do you like that?"

Sounded good to him, but it wasn't Ian's place to say that. "Would you like to do a follow-up interview?"

After a pause, she declined. "I think we've said more than enough already. Still, if we decide to talk to anyone, it will be you. I just hope this is over soon."

"So do I."

After saying goodbye, he checked his e-mail one last time for the night and found a message from Viktor.

Great work, between Judge Wycliff and this baby business. You've outdone yourself, his brother-in-law wrote. Anni and I will be flying to New York on Thursday for a week of business and pleasure. We'd like you to join us. You can charge the ticket to the company.

Ian's fingers froze on the keypad. If Viktor simply wanted a personal reunion, he wouldn't offer to pay for the ticket. That left the matter of the "From the Fire" column. Was the company going to offer it to Ian, or let him down easy?

He'd better be prepared, either way.

On Tuesday morning, with Mark's approval, Jennifer issued a statement that repeated the basic facts of the case from twelve years ago and expressed sympathy for the McCoys. She let Willa release it to the swarms of press in the lobby.

May Chong, the administration secretary, screened reporters' calls to Jennifer's office. Much as she disliked asking staff to cover for her, Jennifer considered it best to stay out of public view.

There'd been no comment from corporate headquarters in Louisville. Perhaps if matters blew over quickly, the whole thing could be ignored.

Still, media reports, which she monitored on the Internet, gave the impression that she'd escaped all the consequences of her actions and gone blithely on her way. Unlike Ian's article, many of the truncated stories glossed over key details, such as saying she "claimed" to have been "under duress" without mentioning that Frank had held her at gunpoint.

At lunchtime she ducked into the day-care center to see Rosalie. The baby burbled happily as Jennifer fed her a bottle. Thank heaven for precious moments like this.

You're her mother now, Sunny had said on the phone yesterday. *I admire the way you've risen above everything you went through. It gives me hope for myself.*

That helped offset some of the cruel e-mails Jennifer had received this morning. People had accused her of everything from getting away with murder—apparently they hadn't read the story very closely—to using her position at the hospital to adopt a baby that should have gone to an infertile couple.

After restoring Rosalie to her crib, she considered skipping lunch, but she was hungry. Besides, she wasn't going to avoid her friends, even though neither of them had contacted her this morning. They'd be expecting to meet her at lunch.

Maybe.

Jennifer's stomach started churning the second she stepped into the cafeteria. Heads swiveled her way, and then the employees averted their gazes. As a conversational buzz arose, she felt like the day she'd returned to high school, determined to finish senior year and earn her diploma. There'd been snide remarks, sneering expressions and utter isolation. Her only consolation had been that the other kids didn't dare taunt her openly. Too intimidated to antagonize a girl who ran around with gun-toting criminals, she'd gathered.

After purchasing a sandwich, Jennifer made her way between the tables. Conversations fell silent as she passed, then resumed in a blur of voices behind her.

Ahead, through the opening to the patio, she spotted Samantha and Lori at a table. Jennifer quailed. She'd never forgotten the moment when she sat down at the table with her best friends in high school, girls she'd shared sleepovers and shopping trips with, and they picked up their trays and moved away.

The two women looked toward her. Gazing at them, Jennifer remembered her first impressions when she'd arrived six months ago. She'd immediately liked Lori's open, kind face. Samantha's features were more pointed and her natural expression sharper, but she'd shown nothing but kindness.

Until now?

Both of them picked up their plates. After a heart-stopping moment, Jennifer realized they were simply clearing space for her.

She started breathing again. This really *wasn't* high school.

As she reached the table, Lori spoke up. "You have got to hear this!"

Jennifer slid into a seat. "Hear what?"

"Tony insists we hold the reception at his house even if Esther's not there," she crowed. "He says she's created enough of a mess and he doesn't want it to affect my wedding. Isn't that sweet?"

"He's a great guy," Jennifer responded. *Thank goodness we're talking about something, anything, other than me.* "That woman's an idiot to risk losing him."

"If they really love each other, things will come together for them," Samantha commented.

Lori didn't look convinced. "I'm out of patience with Esther. Like I said, I understand that my wedding isn't the big issue here, but she's acting as if it doesn't even matter."

"Well, it matters to *us*." Jennifer caught her breath. Was she presuming too much? She wouldn't blame Lori for not wanting the hospital's scarlet woman to march down the aisle ahead of her.

"You're not bailing out on me, are you?" Lori asked. "I'm counting on you and Samantha to be my comaids of honor."

To Jennifer's embarrassment, her eyes burned. "I might cry."

Both of her friends reached over, each cupping one of her hands. "We're on your side," Lori said.

"You were seventeen, and the jerk put a gun to your head," Samantha added. "How dare people blame you for that?"

"And I lost my…" She hadn't meant to reveal that.

Oh, why not? "I was five months pregnant. The crash killed my baby."

Neither of them spoke for a moment. Then Lori said, "I'm so sorry."

"Do those people—the McCoys—know about it?" Samantha asked.

Jennifer shook her head. "Mrs. McCoy's still suffering the aftermath of that crash. I wouldn't feel right making a play for her sympathy."

"Don't be a martyr," the pediatrician responded.

"It's not that bad," she assured them. "Now, let's discuss giving Lori a shower. Isn't that what maids of honor are supposed to do?"

They were nearly finished eating when her cell rang. It was Mark, asking her to come upstairs immediately.

"That doesn't sound good," Samantha commented when Jennifer relayed the information. "I'm coming with you."

"I'd go, too, but we've got patients scheduled. I hope he's not going to get sidetracked." Lori had to pick up the slack when Mark's duties as administrator delayed his obstetrical appointments.

Jennifer didn't answer. She had a bad feeling about this.

Samantha patted her hand again. "Let's go."

They cleared their dishes and headed back. This time, other staff members kept their staring to a minimum. Perhaps they'd already satisfied their curiosity, or more likely they didn't want to risk a glare from the fiery pediatrician.

At the administrative offices, they found Mark pacing. He seemed startled to see Samantha, but ushered them both into his office without comment.

Usually, Jennifer took a moment to enjoy the view through the glass walls of the harbor and, beyond, the vast blue brilliance of the ocean. On a clear day like this, the vista included Catalina Island in the distance.

Today she'd have been satisfied to stare at a blank wall if only she could keep her job.

"Well?" Samantha demanded.

The administrator grimaced. "I just had a difficult conversation with Chandra Yashimoto. Apparently, the corporation's receiving a lot of flak from around the country. She's had angry phone calls and e-mails."

All the warmth flushed out of the room. "She wants me fired?" Jennifer asked.

"If she goes, I'm going, too," Samantha declared.

Stunned at the intensity of her friend's loyalty, Jennifer barely managed to respond. "You can't do that. What about your patients?"

"Nobody's firing anybody if I can help it," Mark said. "However, she ordered me—us—to clean up this mess. She said publicists aren't supposed to create negative publicity, and I have to admit, this could hurt the hospital. You're the public relations expert. Any suggestions?"

The answer that came to Jennifer was almost as bad as getting fired. "I think it's best if I hand in my resignation."

She hadn't counted on Samantha. "Don't be an idiot!"

"Diplomatic as always," Mark muttered.

"You're going to hold a press conference and tell the public about your miscarriage," her friend said.

"No…"

"It might work," conceded the administrator, to whom she'd relayed the whole story. "I hate to put you in such a position, Jennifer, but it does show that you suffered, too. Plus it will give you a chance to respond to some of the more irresponsible claims floating about in cyberspace."

She folded her arms. "If it were just a matter of my privacy, I'd sacrifice that for the hospital's good. After all, it's my job to enhance our reputation, not harm it."

"You can't be worried about protecting the McCoys!" Samantha burst out. "For heaven's sake, you have a right to tell the truth. If that takes some of the wind out of their sails, tough."

"It's more than that." Jennifer instinctively recoiled from using a hospital press conference as a personal appeal for vindication, no matter what the cost to her. "A media event like this would turn the situation into a circus. What do my problems have to do with Safe Harbor as an institution? If I quit, the hospital's protected from any further damage. That would be the honorable thing for me to do."

In Mark's face, she read admiration and a trace of surprise. In Samantha's, she saw only stubbornness.

"What if we held a press conference that *enhanced* the hospital's image?" the pediatrician asked. "I have an idea how we can leverage this to do some actual good."

"Why do I suspect I'm about to be buffaloed into something?" Mark didn't seem to expect an answer.

"I'm listening," Jennifer said.

And tried not to hope too much. Because even Samantha couldn't work miracles.

Chapter Seventeen

Nothing brought you down to earth like a baby, Jennifer mused as she drove home, listening to Rosalie's happy cooing from the rear seat. She'd spent all afternoon setting up the press conference for tomorrow while fending off the media's inquiries about what she planned to announce.

Already, stories had begun circulating on the Web that she intended to resign. Thank goodness that wasn't the case—not yet, anyway. A lot depended on how this presentation went over.

Pulling into the driveway to her condo's parking area, she scanned the street for news vans or anyone loitering about who might be a member of the press. Then she glimpsed one—Ian.

He sat on her porch, tapping away at a netbook perched on his knees. When he spotted her and grinned, her spirits lifted.

After Jennifer parked around back, they met in the central courtyard, where he relieved her of the baby carrier, and they headed toward her unit. "How's my girl?" he asked the baby. "And how's her mom holding up?"

"Surviving." Her stomach rumbled. From the delicious smell, one of the neighbors must be frying chicken.

"I hear you called a press conference."

So that's what brought him here. "You're expecting a preview?"

Ian paused before a row of mailboxes. "Jennifer, I didn't drive to Safe Harbor to ask for favors. I came to see you." There was genuine hurt in his eyes.

"I'm sorry." She sighed. "It's been a rough day."

"Yes, and in large part because of me." He resumed walking. "I'm the guy who put you in the spotlight in the first place."

"I put myself in the spotlight. Nobody forced me to become a publicist."

"Well, that's true."

When she'd begun studying communications, she hadn't thought about the potential implications, Jennifer conceded. Thrilled to discover she had a knack for handling publicity, she'd pursued her classes with enthusiasm. Never had she expected the glare to turn on *her.*

"I figured it was *other* people I'd make famous. Or notorious, as the case may be."

"You still have your job?" Ian waited while she unlocked her door.

"For now." Inside, as they carried Rosalie upstairs, she explained about the decision to reveal her miscarriage. "I realize you already have the information, but please don't release it ahead of time."

"I promised to keep it confidential, and I will, until

you release it. But that doesn't preclude me from working on my story in advance. I'll update it with whatever you say tomorrow."

"So you may still beat your competition by a few minutes," she observed.

"That's the idea."

"Always competitive."

"Which is why they pay me the big bucks," he said wryly. "Note the Rolls-Royce and the designer suit."

"If you get the new position…"

"They'll bump my pay a notch or two. I might even open a savings account." He watched as she tucked the yawning infant into the crib. "Isn't it a little early for bedtime?"

"The day-care lady said she refused to nap." Perhaps the baby had picked up Jennifer's uneasy mood. "I hope she'll catch a few winks while I fix dinner."

"Brought some." He indicated his shoulder bag. "Can't you smell the fried chicken?"

That explained the delicious aroma. "I've been drooling since I ran into you."

"Women tell me that all the time."

She laughed. "Competitive *and* modest."

"I decided I've mooched more than enough of your food." He peered out the window. "Gorgeous sunset."

Jennifer moved closer and followed his line of sight. "Oh, it's lovely. I'd like to bring some of those colors inside the room—repaint the walls. This beige is way too bland."

"The walls *are* a little bare," he agreed.

"And I'll order blowups of the photos we had taken." The photographer had captured adorable shots of Rosalie alone and in Jennifer's arms. "As she grows, I'd like to create a memory wall."

"I wish I could be here." Ian's voice sounded hoarse. "Damn it, I hate having to leave."

"I hate it, too."

For an instant, neither of them moved, and then they reached for each other. Ian's mouth explored hers lovingly, not seeking anything, not urging her to the bedroom, simply connecting them.

With a vast sense of rightness, Jennifer melted into the man she loved. Yes, loved. Without realizing it and without her consent, she'd fallen for this fellow. So what if he wasn't going to figure into her future or be around to pick up the pieces if the press conference tomorrow failed? He was here now.

At last he released her. "I hate to admit it, but I'm starving."

"Me, too." Pleased to see that the baby had drifted off, she took Ian's hand and led him downstairs to dinner.

THE LAST TIME IAN had visited this wood-paneled auditorium with its comfortably tiered seats, he'd been looking for a story. Today, he wished this story would go away.

The people jamming the room, filling the seats and cramming the aisles with their minicams and laptops and cell phones at the ready, seemed like intruders. They skimmed the surface, jumping from sound bite to sound bite.

Like I used to do. And might have to again, if he didn't land the column.

Last night, after he and Jennifer made love, they'd lain awake for hours, talking. He'd told her about being summoned to New York and his doubts about whether he had landed the promotion. She'd insisted that Flash News/Global would be crazy to give it to anyone else.

As soon as he filed his story today, he'd grab his few possessions and catch a flight to New York. From there, he'd likely head for his next base of operations, wherever that might be.

It might be many months, or longer, before he'd return. Months during which Rosalie would learn to crawl and babble, walk and talk. Months during which Jennifer would move on, perhaps meet someone new.

But no matter how much Ian yearned to be with her, he couldn't live a half life. He would never be satisfied with an ordinary job, with a career that failed to make a difference in the world.

Pierre, who lingered close to the stage preparing to video the proceedings, seemed happy enough hanging around Los Angeles, capturing whatever news broke locally. Sometimes it was big news, Ian conceded, but mostly little stuff. Celebrity gossip, criminal proceedings—much like what he'd pursued these past few weeks.

Rewarding at times. Stultifying at others.

All that remained today was to listen to these now-familiar people who were strolling onto the stage—Dr. Rayburn, Dr. Forrest and Jennifer—confirm what he already knew about her past. A few updates to his prepared story and… Wait a minute. What was Samantha's role in today's announcement?

Ian took a deep breath as Jennifer stepped to the microphone. Across the auditorium the murmur of voices hushed.

"Thanks for coming," she told the press. *As if you could have kept them away with a shotgun.* "We have two reasons for calling this press conference. The first is personal, and the second is because my employers at Safe Harbor Medical Center believe that some good ought to come out of tragedy."

She proceeded to outline the facts of the robbery, including Frank's coercion. When she revealed that she'd been pregnant and described awakening to discover she'd lost the baby, she didn't even try to stem her tears.

"I'm not telling you this so you can choose sides about who to feel sorry for. The McCoy family suffered terribly, and I want to apologize to them. If I'd exercised better judgment about who I dated, if I'd tried to escape instead of following his commands, maybe I could have prevented what happened," she said. "It's too late to go back, but it isn't too late to change the future."

Rising, Samantha moved to a second microphone. Ian leaned forward, curious.

"At Safe Harbor we've seen a lot of confused, hurting young women in the past few weeks, as you all know," the pediatrician said. "I'm delighted to announce plans for a counseling clinic to help women deal with issues of fertility, pregnancy and early child care. This press conference marks the start of a fundraising campaign so that we can offer services to anyone who needs them. We're going to call it the Edward Serra Memorial Clinic, after the baby who died in the accident."

Jennifer's mouth fell open. "You're what?"

This wasn't part of the script, Ian realized with a lump in his throat.

Dr. Rayburn joined the women to express the administration's support for the new endeavor, and then members of the press began throwing out questions. In their voices Ian heard sympathy and interest in place of hostility. Things had worked out better than he could have anticipated.

Then, as he turned to slip out, he observed two people at the back, staring toward the stage. With a jolt, he recognized Andrea and John McCoy.

What on earth were they doing here?

UNTIL THE LATEST UPROAR, Medical Center Management would have instantly rejected Samantha's proposal to open a charitable clinic, Jennifer had no doubt. Even so, it had taken all of Mark's powers to persuade Chandra and her superiors that this announcement offered the hospital a much-needed goodwill boost in the public's eye.

They'd pulled it off. Blunted the criticism of Jennifer personally, and restored Safe Harbor's good name.

The decision to name the clinic after her lost son was a complete surprise. The recognition that he hadn't died in vain filled Jennifer with bittersweet elation.

She allowed her gaze to drift to Ian in the back of the auditorium. Who was that middle-aged couple standing near him? There was something familiar about the woman leaning on a cane and the stoop-shouldered man....

The reporters' questions and Mark's and Samantha's answers faded from Jennifer's awareness. Oh, heavens. She hadn't seen these people in twelve years. And now...had they come to tell her off personally, in public?

She supposed she should wrap up this session fast, before they summoned the courage to speak out. Ian had claimed the pair weren't intent on revenge, but suppose they'd changed their minds? If they turned the press conference into a forum for their personal vendetta, they could cause immense damage. Not only to her, but also to the fundraising efforts for the new clinic.

Too late. They'd begun making their way up the center aisle, drawing every eye. Cameras swung their way, and in the buzz from the floor, Jennifer caught the name McCoy. Everyone, it seemed, had identified them as the wronged couple.

On the stage, Mark shot her a questioning look. Perhaps she could still try to cut them off, but those poor people. Every painful step they took reminded her of what they'd suffered.

Impulsively Jennifer hurried down the steps and went to meet them. "There's a ramp to the side if you need it," she told Andrea.

In the woman's lined face Jennifer saw the harsh toll the years had taken. Not that Andrea had been in great shape at the trial, either; too badly injured to sit for long periods, she'd been able to spend only a few minutes on the witness stand.

John, however, had attended every single court session after he completed his testimony. In the courtroom, whenever Jennifer had glanced his way, his rage-filled expression had scorched her. At Frank's sentencing, his fury had coalesced into pure hatred. She'd actually stepped backward in fear that the man might attack her.

Now, with an effort, she forced herself to meet his gaze. His eyes glimmered. Could those be tears?

"We didn't know about the baby." His wife put a

hand on Jennifer's arm. "We didn't realize how much you'd lost."

"It strikes me that you were the same age that our daughter is today," John McCoy added ruefully. "You were just a kid."

"Can you ever forgive me?" Jennifer asked.

"I'm only sorry we've wasted all these years holding on to our anger." He raised his voice, loud enough for the reporters to hear. "Andrea and I would like to make the first donation to the Edward Serra Memorial Clinic."

"This clinic is a wonderful idea," Andrea added. "I always felt there had to be a reason for us to endure so much."

Careful not to jostle the frail woman, Jennifer hugged her. Before she knew it, she was hugging John, too. "I'm sorry," she kept saying, over and over.

Cameras flashed. Videocams whirred. When her vision cleared enough to make out the stage, Mark and Samantha were beaming.

Amazingly, everything had turned out all right.

Except that, as more questions flew and reporters closed in, Ian gave her a farewell tilt of the head and strode from the room. No doubt eager to file his story, but as he'd explained earlier, also on a tight deadline to make his flight out of LAX.

Gone.

They'd said goodbye this morning. She supposed that, with phones and e-mail and text messages, the world had become a small place.

Yet it remained infinitely vast.

How ironic that, at the moment when the wounds of

twelve years ago were finally beginning to heal, Ian had ripped a hole in her heart. A hole that she suspected she would spend the rest of her life trying to fill.

But he'd given her so much. Without him, this reconciliation wouldn't have been possible.

After wiping her cheeks, Jennifer gratefully accompanied John and Andrea McCoy to the stage. She still had a job to do.

And she wished Ian the best with his, wherever in the world it might take him.

Chapter Eighteen

On his first morning in New York, Ian slept late, enjoying the comfort of his hotel room. It might be modest by five-star luxury standards, but it put the L.A. motel to shame.

A firm mattress with extralarge pillows. Heavy curtains that blocked the light. A bathroom large enough so he didn't bump into things, with extra toiletries and thick, soft towels.

Besides, what else did he have to do? He wasn't scheduled to see Viktor and Anni until dinnertime, and felt no inclination to play tourist, since he'd attended university in New York and visited many times since. Shopping held little interest for a man who had nowhere to put possessions, and he'd long ago lost touch with his college classmates.

As he showered, Ian tried to picture what Jennifer might be doing. Ten o'clock in the east meant seven in California. He visualized her rocking in the nursery chair, feeding Rosalie a bottle while mentally redecorating the room. And taking comfort in the results of the press conference.

The heartwarming reconciliation had made the national and international news. On a TV screen at the L.A. airport, Ian had glimpsed Jennifer embracing the McCoys, just as he'd seen them in person a short while earlier. On the Internet, his article and Pierre's images—both video and JPEG—were everywhere.

He toweled off and willed his brain to shift into "here and now" mode. Usually, once he wrapped up loose ends and left a locale, he immediately snapped back to his normal state of being ready for action.

Instead, he continued mentally following Jennifer through her morning routine. Putting on makeup, dressing Rosalie…

The phone rang. He grabbed it. "Martin."

"Hey, Ian." A female voice, intimately familiar, but not Jennifer's. Ian's mouth curled with instant recognition.

"Yo, Anni. In town already?" Viktor hadn't mentioned their arrival time, only that they were staying at the same hotel.

"And hungry. Want to meet me in the coffee shop? My hubby's gone to work and left me all alone."

"You bet." Ian wished he and his twin hadn't drifted so far apart these past few years. They barely saw each other once or twice a year, and almost always surrounded by others.

Such distance was inevitable, he supposed, but a far cry from their closeness while growing up. Not only had they shared their mother's womb, they'd been best friends and a constant source of support during the family's frequent relocations.

It was to him rather than their mother that Anni had confided her secret crushes on boys. And he'd turned to her for advice on how to win dates with girls, back in those days when most had considered him a skinny, overly intellectual geek.

They'd shared their ambitions, as well. Both had gone to college in the New York area and had looked forward to their occasional lunch meetings, when they'd laughed, consoled each other on disappointments and spun wonderful dreams.

Anticipation quickening, he gathered a few things and hurried downstairs. In the lobby, he heard the ding of the adjacent elevator and turned to see Anni exiting at almost the same instant. Like him, she carried a small shopping bag.

Birthday gifts. The big date wasn't till next month, but they weren't likely to see each other again that soon.

Big hug. Paper rustled, and the scent of peppermint filled the air. Anni loved the stuff.

Ian stood back. "You look radiant."

She grinned up at him. Even discounting the obvious gender difference, they were far from identical: she stood a few inches shorter, and had chin-length hair a shade darker than his. Anni used to complain that she wouldn't have minded inheriting the blond locks, but instead got stuck with the same narrowly chiseled face, which suited him, but in her opinion, made her look gaunt. Well, she'd rounded out, and to Ian's eye she looked fabulous.

"Whoa! You aren't pregnant, are you?" he guessed.

His sister made a face. "Typical male. The only thing that could make a woman glow is fertility, right? Well, hah! I sold a short story, that's what." She named a prestigious British literary magazine.

"Good for you!" He strolled beside her to the coffee

shop, their gaits perfectly matched despite the difference in height.

After placing orders for crisp bacon and eggs over easy—he chose rye toast, though, and she preferred whole wheat—they exchanged shopping bags. "Happy birthday!" they said in unison.

Each poked through the wrappings. Anni first pulled out two books wrapped in balloon-themed paper. "For the girls," Ian explained. "The bookseller raved about them, and they're new, so I took a chance that you don't have them already."

"That's so sweet." Anni tucked them away for her daughters to unwrap. "You go next."

He opened his gift. Inside the boxful of tissue paper nestled a slim leather wallet, key chain, business card holder and money clip, all worked with a design of the moon and stars.

"For the man who has everything and needs something to put it in," his twin announced.

"They're stunning. Mind if I ask why the celestial theme?"

"Because you've always wanted the moon and I know you'll keep on reaching for the stars, no matter what happens," Anni said.

He felt a twinge of uneasiness. *No matter what happens.* Did that mean he hadn't won the promotion? Still, it seemed foolish to read in too much. "Perfect choice. These are elegant, and my old wallet's nearly worn out. Now open yours."

With a wriggle of anticipation, his twin unwrapped the items he'd selected: a beautifully bound blank book and a fountain pen.

"To write your novel," Ian said. Anni had always preferred composing longhand rather than on the computer. "Or more short stories."

She ran a finger over the embossed binding. "I love it. Thank you."

When a wing of hair tumbled across her cheek, Ian reached across the table and brushed it into place. "You look happy. I trust things are going well with Viktor and the girls."

"Better than I had any right to expect." She stared down at the blank book in her hands.

"What does that mean?"

The waitress arrived with their food, and Anni delayed her answer until they were alone again. "This wasn't exactly the life I chose," she admitted as she sprinkled salt on her eggs. "That's what I've been writing about in my stories. Choices and happenstance and where life takes us."

"What exactly didn't you choose?" He reached for the salt as soon as she finished with it.

"After my marriage I planned to keep on reporting full-time at least until my late thirties," his sister said. "Then I got pregnant."

"That was an accident?" He'd never had an inkling.

Anni nodded. "At first I wasn't sure what to do. After a while I reconciled to the fact that sometimes you have to compromise. When Bethany was born, the truth finally hit me."

"That a baby is a miracle?" Ian asked.

"Well, sure, although I never expected to hear that from you," his twin teased. "But also that I was going to get older whether I moved in all the right circles, or stayed in a small circle of love. I am who I am, and I've got the talents I've got. In the end, the best use of my abilities is whatever makes me and the people I care about fulfilled and happy. So here I am, and no regrets. Not one."

"I'm glad," Ian told her. "Do you suppose they have any cayenne?"

She pulled a small container from her purse. "I always carry some with me." They took turns peppering their eggs.

As he ate, Ian mulled this unexpected revelation about his sister. He'd never suspected that events, rather than choice, had shaped the course of her life. Yet she did seem more than merely contented.

At the same time, he couldn't deny a growing sense of disquiet at her bringing up the subject of accepting whatever hand fate dealt you. Had she sprung this revelation by chance, or was she trying to prepare him for a letdown?

She'd struck a chord that resonated with him, Ian had to admit. He *was* getting older, and the adventure of flitting from one post to another had begun losing its thrill. If he didn't land the column, what lay ahead? Certainly he didn't want to go on this way indefinitely.

He ought to make the best of his few days in New York. It never hurt to plant a few seeds that might bear fruit later. Holding that thought, he returned his focus to his sister.

For the rest of the meal, he updated her about his experiences in California. Although he skimmed over his feelings for Jennifer, he suspected Anni had a good idea of how matters lay. She didn't press for details, though.

"I'm planning to hit the art museums this afternoon," she said when they'd finished eating. "Want to come with me?"

"Actually, I have plans." He deliberately left the matter vague, partly because the plans had just begun to take shape in his mind.

"I'll see you tonight, then." Anni tucked her blank book into the gift bag.

"I can hardly wait."

Actually, Ian didn't mean to wait at all. He intended to stay very, very busy.

"THIS IS THE LIFE." Lori leaned back in the hand-carved white recliner. "Esther must be out of her mind. I can't imagine why she'd want to work a zillion hours a week in Washington when she could be here."

Sunlight streamed through the artfully designed patio cover, turning the outdoor kitchen and lounge area into a Mediterranean fantasy. Nearby, water splashed between rocks and ferns into a pool. Tony Franco's house was going to be the perfect setting for the reception—possibly even more perfect without its opinionated mistress, in Jennifer's opinion.

"Wasn't Esther also working a zillion hours a week at the district attorney's office?" she asked.

"Well, who forced her to do that?" Lori glanced over at their companion. "As usual, no use trying to get a response out of Sam."

"Be with you in a minute." Samantha tapped buttons on her Smartphone. The last time Jennifer checked, she'd been researching counseling centers to see how they organized their staff and services.

The two days since the press conference had been

crammed with planning for the Edward Serra Memorial Clinic. Between consulting with Samantha about fund-raising and dealing with the press, Jennifer had barely had a spare moment.

Even so, memories of Ian invaded her thoughts at random moments—while she cradled Rosalie, while she ate breakfast, whenever she crossed the hospital lobby.

In a perverse way, she wished he'd finish whatever business he was conducting in New York and head to his next assignment. Once she knew for certain he wasn't coming back—not that she put much stock in that possibility—maybe she could put him in the past once and for all.

They'd exchanged e-mails on Friday, but all he'd said was that he was incredibly busy and would fill her in later. Reluctant to intrude, she'd refrained from phoning, and he hadn't called her.

Out of sight, out of mind. On his part, anyway. That seemed the most likely explanation.

"Jared asked me to move in with him," Lori said. "Isn't that cool?"

A spurt of envy dismayed Jennifer. She wanted to be glad for her friend, not envious. "Good for you."

"That's hardly a surprise," murmured Samantha. "You guys *are* getting married."

"I know, but since he hadn't said anything, I assumed he wanted to wait. Of course, now I have to deal with logistics." Her freckled nose scrunched. "I've got so much stuff in my apartment."

"Isn't his house a three-bedroom?" Jennifer asked. "That's one bedroom and two offices. That's plenty of room."

"I hadn't thought of it that way." Lori stretched. "I'm so tired, my brain's just not functioning properly."

"Yeah, we really worked our butts off today," Samantha said without removing her gaze from the device. "Oh, wait—we were tasting cakes."

"That's *work,*" Lori joked. "Anyway, we spent nearly an hour deciding where to set up the tables and stuff for the reception. No wonder I'm exhausted."

Jennifer felt tired, too, less from the planning than from struggling not to fantasize about how it might feel to marry the man of her dreams. The man who, these past few weeks, had gone from a vague fantasy to a painfully beloved reality.

Stop torturing yourself. But how was she supposed to do that? Even though acting pushy went against every instinct, she couldn't seem to let go until she knew for sure what Ian's plans were.

From the far side of the house, she heard a heavy door swing shut. Tony, who'd given Lori a key so she and her attendants could examine the premises, must be back from his golf game.

The noise woke Rosalie, who let out a cry from the baby carrier. "Time to go home." Jennifer tried not to show her relief, because much as she enjoyed her friends' company, she suddenly couldn't wait to leave.

And get this over with.

The next quarter hour passed in a fever of impatience. Aware that Rosalie reflected her moods, Jennifer struggled to slow her breathing and focus on the moment. Pack up the diaper bag, chat politely with Tony, say goodbye to her friends. Strap the baby in the car and head home.

At the condo, she noted that it was four o'clock, which meant seven in New York. Ian might have gone to dinner, but propelled by sheer nerves, Jennifer dialed his number.

The call went directly to voice mail. No way was she leaving a message.

She tried again at five. Still no luck.

He'd mentioned the hotel where he was booked, so she called the operator, who put her through to his room. The phone rang twice.

"Hello?" said a woman's voice.

In a sudden panic, Jennifer nearly hung up, but that would be rude. Besides, she owed him the benefit of the doubt. "Hi. Is Ian there?"

"He's in the shower. I could have him call you back."

Embarrassment flooded her. He certainly hadn't wasted a moment finding companionship. "That won't be necessary."

"Is this Jennifer?"

The sound of her name startled her. "Yes?"

"This is his sister, Anni. He told me about you."

His sister. Of course. She should have trusted him, Jennifer thought, ashamed of jumping to conclusions. "Good things, I hope."

"Absolutely. I'm sorry about answering the phone— that probably gave you a start. My brother and I took in a concert this afternoon, and we're meeting my husband in a few minutes. I'll have him call as soon as he can."

"It isn't urgent." In truth, she didn't see how she could bear to wait another minute to find out about Ian's future. "I just wondered... He mentioned a possible promotion...."

"Oh, he got it," Anni said. "Isn't that wonderful? It's so nice of you to be concerned."

Disappointment arrowed through Jennifer. Subconsciously, she realized, she'd been hoping that if the column didn't materialize, Ian might request an assignment to the L.A. bureau. Now he'd be off to the ends of the earth.

Yet she felt glad for him, too. This job was his dream, and he deserved it. "He's a great guy. I'm sure he'll do brilliantly."

"He always does." Pride bloomed in his sister's voice. "Listen, I'll tell him you called. And I'll give him your congratulations."

"Thanks."

He didn't call, though. Not that night and not the next day. Nor any day that week.

It wasn't the response Jennifer had hoped for, but his silence told the whole story. Ian had moved on.

She could hardly hold that against him. He'd broken no promises. The excitement of his new position surely overshadowed the few weeks they'd spent together.

And thanks to him, she had half of her dream. Every day her bond with Rosalie deepened. Watching the little one's small advances—her strengthening body control, her growing interest in activities around her—providing an endless source of joy.

Maybe someday the right man would come along, a man whose dreams of home and family matched hers. Just because she couldn't have that with Ian didn't mean she was giving up.

Chapter Nineteen

A brisk breeze whipped Ian's hair and the salty air stung his cheeks as he crossed the quay. Had the weather changed in the ten days he'd been gone, or was it always this cool by the ocean?

He'd stopped by Jennifer's condo, but found no one home. His own fault; he should have called. So he'd taken a chance that she was following her usual routine of walking with her friends on Saturday mornings, and sure enough, through the coffee shop window up ahead, he saw Samantha sitting at a table. Only the back of Jennifer's head was visible, dark hair in its usual knot, tendrils teasing at her neck.

A hot burst of longing drove off the chill. If only he could banish everything else, just be alone with her. But there was too much at stake for him to rush this.

Ian's hands felt stiff. Nerves, he supposed. Odd, considering that he confronted people and asked questions for a living. This was different, though. At all kinds of levels.

That evening a week ago, when Anni gave him Jennifer's message, he'd been in too much of a hurry to return the call immediately. Later he hadn't felt ready to say anything until he put the pieces together and made sure they fit.

He still lacked the final piece. For that, he needed to talk to Jennifer in person.

Ian held the coffee shop door for a pair of older ladies, then stepped inside. Seeing Samantha's face register recognition, he raised a hand in greeting.

When Jennifer swung around, sunlight through the window burnished her skin to velvet. Her eyes were luminous, and her lips parted in surprise. But the welcoming smile he'd anticipated failed to appear.

She had a right to be annoyed, he reflected, and paused by the stroller. "Hey, Rosalie." The baby peeked upward uncertainly. "Yeah, it's me. How's my favorite baby?"

She beamed. *Somebody* was glad to see him, at least.

"Okay if I join you ladies?" He decided not to bother fetching a cup of coffee. Too much of a delay.

Jennifer indicated an empty chair. She still didn't speak.

"Is this a personal conversation?" Samantha asked. "I can leave."

"Actually, it includes you." He glanced around. "Isn't there a third member of this band of sisters?"

"Lori's out with her fiancé today." Jennifer found her voice at last. Her gaze barely flicked over him, though. "Ian, what's this about?"

No sense beating around the bush. "It concerns a book I plan to write. On women and babies and the issues they face in today's changing landscape. Fertility, adoption, surrogates, women who have to relinquish babies, women who adopt them."

"Fantastic!" Samantha said. "Can I be part of this?"

"Absolutely."

"A book?" A pucker formed between Jennifer's shapely brows. "What happened to the Flash News/ Global promotion?"

"Before I knew whether I'd landed it or not, I decided to lay a little groundwork for the future." The explanation poured out, more or less as he'd mentally rehearsed it on the long flight west. "As long as I was in New York, I contacted a friend's agent. He'd seen the video and read my stories about you and Rosalie. He got very excited, declared it was timely and that I already had the public's interest, and we should strike while the iron was hot."

Ian hoped this didn't sound opportunistic. He couldn't read much in Jennifer's expression. He wouldn't blame her for being angry that he hadn't called.

"Ian, you didn't propose a book that involves me, did you?" She balled her napkin into a wad. "I've already had more exposure than I want."

"The book isn't exactly about you, but your story would serve as a jumping-off point," he admitted. "Part of the proceeds would go to the clinic, of course."

"There's a lot that desperately needs to be written on this subject," Samantha commented. "I could help point you in the right direction."

Since Jennifer remained pensive, Ian filled in more blanks. "The agent set up pitch sessions. That's what I was doing all week. I hadn't realized how much I cared about this topic until I started talking to editors. Ideas just tumbled out of me."

"You found a publisher?" Jennifer asked.

"We haven't signed a contract yet, but we've tentatively agreed on terms," Ian told her.

"What if I say no?"

That was a question he'd asked the agent and the editor. "Legally, I don't require your permission," he conceded. "You already gave me the right to use the material from our interviews, and that covers the basics. But I won't go against your wishes, and the book wouldn't be nearly as good without your continuing input."

"You'd turn this down and go back to reporting?" she asked dubiously.

"Viktor gave me until Monday to decide whether to take the promotion," Ian said. "And the publisher understands that I won't proceed without your consent. This really is up to you."

The book wasn't the only issue at stake. But he refused to do anything that might seem manipulative, and that included using their personal connection to win her approval. She had every right to protect her privacy.

"Is this really what you want?" she asked at last. "What about roving the globe, digging out hard truths? I thought that was your dream."

"This is my dream *now.*" He hesitated. "Could we continue this conversation at your place? No offense, Dr. Forrest. I'm glad to know I'll have your support if we proceed with this."

"It would be my pleasure." She glanced at Jennifer and pressed her lips together, as if biting back arguments she longed to present. Instead, she confined her response to a simple "Do whatever you deem best."

As Jennifer rose, Ian held himself in check, as well. Every instinct urged him to tease the sadness from the corners of her mouth and tell her how empty New York—the entire planet—felt without her.

But he respected her too much to do that. The firestorm of publicity that was only beginning to fade would reignite when this book hit the stores. It might affect her future in any number of ways.

The fact that he yearned to be part of that future would have to wait.

JENNIFER DIDN'T SEE HOW she could bear this. For the past week she'd tried to push Ian out of her mind, to accept that their brief involvement had ended forever. Now he'd returned, but for the wrong reasons.

If she turned him down, he'd fly off to write his column. If she agreed, he'd stay—for a while. And after he left, she'd be alone again and even more deeply in love, if that was possible.

As soon as she'd seen him in the coffee shop, his nearness had blotted out everyone and everything else. For a blinding instant she'd been tempted to run straight to him. Thank goodness she hadn't.

In the living room she set Rosalie where the baby could watch them. The infant seemed happiest when observing people and movement.

Ian knelt by the carrier. "When did she start doing that?"

"Doing what?"

"Flexing her hands. See? It's like she's practicing her grip." He peered closely, and received a poke in the nose for his pains. "Hey! Was that deliberate?"

"I don't know," Jennifer admitted. "Ian, let's get this over with."

Uncertainty filled his gaze. That was an emotion she'd never associated with him. "All right."

"I'll go straight to the point. I can't do this," she said.

He sank onto the couch as if his legs refused to hold him. "I understand." His voice had a flat, stunned quality.

Despite her sympathy, Jennifer felt a surge of anger. Why did he have to put her in this position? "I hate throwing cold water on your dreams, but what about mine? Sooner or later, you'll be gone. My heart isn't made of steel, Ian. I want more than you can give me."

He frowned. "Let's get back to that part about me being gone. I never said—"

"Oh, come on. Once this book is done, you'll crave a new challenge, and you won't find it here." Jennifer paced across the room. "Let me tell you my dream. It involves a man who wakes up with me in the morning and goes to sleep with me at night."

"I can do that."

"For a while, maybe. But can you be here for my daughter as she grows into a woman? Can you be a full-time whatever-you-are and a full-time husband and father at the same time? That isn't you, Ian." She hugged herself tightly, trying to contain the pain.

"I think it is."

She hadn't expected that answer. But it fell short. "You *think* so?"

The intensity of his gaze nearly swept her away. "I've learned a lot these past few weeks about who I am. For now, this book is what I want to write. After that, I can't promise I'll be here every morning and every evening, but in the ways that count, I will always be here for you. Will you give me a chance, Jennifer?"

"*I will always be here for you.*" Now it was *her* knees that felt shaky. She stopped pacing and perched gingerly beside Ian. "I don't see how I can be satisfied with a long-distance relationship. I want a family, not a warm phone."

His shoulder brushed hers as he leaned forward earnestly. "Life is messy, Jen. Take passing up the promotion—not to mention leaving my job. I still don't know one hundred percent that this is the perfect route for my career. But I am one hundred percent certain that you're the right woman for me and that Rosalie was meant to be my daughter."

Was she truly hearing this? Could the elusive, charismatic Ian Martin be making a commitment to *her?*

"Will you accept me as I am, accept a future with me, even though I may not be exactly what you'd planned on?" he pressed. "I promise one thing. You will always be the woman I love."

"When the book is finished—"

"I'll write another book. The editor and I discussed a whole series about medical advances that affect people's daily lives. Maybe sometimes I'll have to be gone doing research, but I'll always come home. If you'll marry me. Will you, Jennifer?"

She gripped the edge of the couch, feeling the texture of the fabric to make sure this was real. Not a fantasy. Not a dream.

They'd be running a risk, both of them. Ian's restless energy, his zest, his ambition would never let him become the steady sort of husband she'd imagined. But they were also part of the reason she'd fallen in love with him.

She wasn't a helpless girl anymore, Jennifer saw. She had the strength to match this man at every step. The strength to enjoy their times together, and create a private world with him and Rosalie that would sustain her when he was away.

She gazed at his loving, honest face and said, "Yes."

For a moment neither of them moved. Then he pulled her close and kissed her mouth, her cheeks, her forehead

"I love you so much," Ian whispered. "I hardly remember what I was before we met."

"Impossibly handsome," Jennifer answered promptly. "Also arrogant and pushy."

"Could you engrave that on my wedding ring? 'I love you because you're impossibly handsome, arrogant and pushy'?"

"It would never fit," she said.

"Well, there goes that idea." Ian grinned. Darned if he didn't have the most delicious mouth. "Oh! I nearly forgot your present."

"You brought me a present?"

"It's in the car. Be right back."

He whipped out, leaving the door ajar. Jennifer peeked at Rosalie, who gazed back wide-eyed. "Not many babies get to watch their daddies propose to their mommies," she told the infant.

The little girl sighed. A born romantic, obviously.

A trunk slammed and Ian reappeared, carrying a paper-covered rectangle. "It's for the nursery. Let's unveil it upstairs."

Bemused, Jennifer picked up the baby and followed. Striding ahead eagerly, Ian reached the room first and, when she entered, stood staring at the two photos she'd hung a few days ago.

One showed Rosalie, a tiny pink bow in her tuft of hair, lolling against a bunny-shaped cushion. In the other, Jennifer sat on a velvet rug, cradling the infant and gazing up at the camera.

"You both look angelic." Ian swallowed. "What was in your mind when the photographer took that shot?"

She was almost embarrassed to reveal it. "You."

"Really?"

"He asked me to visualize someone I loved." For an instant her heart had leaped ahead of her judgment.

"I'll remember that every time I look at it. Did you have wallet prints made? I'd like to carry one around."

"Of course." She put the baby in the crib. "May I open my present now?"

"By all means."

She pulled off the wrapping and removed a padded layer. The frame appeared the perfect size to hang next to the others, but what…

Jennifer's breath caught at the image of a cherubic infant rising from a half eggshell, as if newly hatched. "It's adorable!" This was not only a photo, but a work of art.

"The gallery said it symbolizes rebirth," Ian murmured, hugging her from behind. "Perfect for our fresh start, eh?"

Jennifer's practical side intervened. "This must have cost a fortune!"

"No more than the diamond earrings I wanted to buy, to go with the diamond ring we're going to pick out," he told her.

"I'd much rather have this than earrings." She rested her head against his chest, feeling utterly safe and sheltered.

"Can we stay here forever?" Ian's words rumbled through her. "Just bring in a preacher and family members and guests. We could cram a dozen or so people into the room, don't you agree?"

"I know a couple of bridesmaids' dresses we could borrow." Jennifer smiled at the silly, endearing image of staging a wedding in the nursery. "I already spent half a day tasting cakes. What do you say to chocolate raspberry?"

"Mmm."

"We could honeymoon down the hall." Mischievously she added, "How about holding a rehearsal right now?"

"I vote for that," he said. "Although I never heard of couples rehearsing their honeymoons."

"We'll start a new tradition." She swung around, straight into his arms. "Of course, we have to keep on rehearsing until we get it right."

Blue fire lit his eyes. "Like I said, I've always had the most amazing luck."

And so, Jennifer thought as they went down the hall to inaugurate their life together, did she.

* * * * *

Watch for more stories set at Safe Harbor Medical!
THE MOMMY CONTRACT
by Jacqueline Diamond
arrives in bookstores August 2010,
only from Harlequin American Romance.

Rancher Ramsey Westmoreland's
temporary cook is way too attractive for his liking.
Little does he know Chloe Burton
came to his ranch with another agenda entirely....

That man across the street had to be, without a doubt, the most handsome man she'd ever seen.

Chloe Burton's pulse beat rhythmically as he stopped to talk to another man in front of a feed store. He was tall, dark and every inch of sexy—from his Stetson to the well-worn leather boots on his feet. And from the way his jeans and Western shirt fit his broad muscular shoulders, it was quite obvious he had everything it took to separate the men from the boys. The combination was enough to corrupt any woman's mind and had her weakening even from a distance. Her body felt flushed. It was hot. Unsettled.

Over the past year the only male who had gotten her time and attention had been the e-mail. That was simply pathetic, especially since now she was practically drooling simply at the sight of a man. Even his stance—both hands in his jeans pockets, legs braced apart, was a pose she would carry to her dreams.

And he was smiling, evidently enjoying the conversation being exchanged. He had dimples, incredibly sexy dimples in not one but both cheeks.

"What are you staring at, Clo?"

Chloe nearly jumped. She'd forgotten she had a

lunch date. She glanced over the table at her best friend from college, Lucia Conyers.

"Take a look at that man across the street in the blue shirt, Lucia. Will he not be perfect for Denver's first issue of *Simply Irresistible* or what?" Chloe asked with so much excitement she almost couldn't stand it.

She was the owner of *Simply Irresistible*, a magazine for today's up-and-coming woman. Their once-a-year Irresistible Man cover, which highlighted a man the magazine felt deserved the honor, had increased sales enough for Chloe to open a Denver office.

When Lucia didn't say anything but kept staring, Chloe's smile widened. "Well?"

Lucia glanced across the booth at her. "Since you asked, I'll tell you what I see. One of the Westmorelands—Ramsey Westmoreland. And yes, he'd be perfect for the cover, but he won't do it."

Chloe raised a brow. "He'd get paid for his services, of course."

Lucia laughed and shook her head. "Getting paid won't be the issue, Clo—Ramsey is one of the wealthiest sheep ranchers in this part of Colorado. But everyone knows what a private person he is. Trust me—he won't do it."

Chloe couldn't help but smile. The man was the epitome of what she was looking for in a magazine cover and she was determined that whatever it took, he would be it.

"Umm, I don't like that look on your face, Chloe. I've seen it before and know exactly what it means."

She watched as Ramsey Westmoreland entered the store with a swagger that made her almost breathless. She *would* be seeing him again.

Look for Silhouette Desire's
HOT WESTMORELAND NIGHTS
by Brenda Jackson,
available March 9 wherever books are sold.

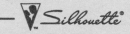

SPECIAL EDITION

FROM *USA TODAY* BESTSELLING AUTHOR
CHRISTINE RIMMER

A BRIDE FOR JERICHO BRAVO

Marnie Jones had long ago buried her wild-child
impulses and opted to be "safe," romantically
speaking. But one look at born rebel Jericho Bravo
and she began to wonder if her thrill-seeking side
was about to be revived. Because if ever there was
a man worth taking a chance on, there he was,
right within her grasp....

*Available in March
wherever books are sold.*

HARLEQUIN
Ambassadors

Want to share your passion for reading Harlequin® Books?

Become a Harlequin Ambassador!

Harlequin Ambassadors are a group of passionate and well-connected readers who are willing to share their joy of reading Harlequin® books with family and friends.

You'll be sent all the tools you need to spark great conversation, including free books!

All we ask is that you share the romance with your friends and family!

You'll also be invited to have a say in new book ideas and exchange opinions with women just like you!

To see if you qualify* to be a Harlequin Ambassador, please visit www.HarlequinAmbassadors.com.

*Please note that not everyone who applies to be a Harlequin Ambassador will qualify. For more information please visit www.HarlequinAmbassadors.com.

Thank you for your participation.

BAP09BPA

REQUEST YOUR FREE BOOKS!

2 FREE NOVELS PLUS 2 FREE GIFTS!

HARLEQUIN®

American ★ Romance®

Love, Home & Happiness!

YES! Please send me 2 FREE Harlequin® American Romance® novels and my 2 FREE gifts (gifts are worth about $10). After receiving them, if I don't wish to receive any more books, I can return the shipping statement marked "cancel." If I don't cancel, I will receive 4 brand-new novels every month and be billed just $4.24 per book in the U.S. or $4.99 per book in Canada. That's a saving of close to 15% off the cover price! It's quite a bargain! Shipping and handling is just 50¢ per book in the U.S. and 75¢ per book in Canada.* I understand that accepting the 2 free books and gifts places me under no obligation to buy anything. I can always return a shipment and cancel at any time. Even if I never buy another book from Harlequin, the two free books and gifts are mine to keep forever.

154 HDN E4CC   354 HDN E4CN

Name	(PLEASE PRINT)

Address	Apt. #

City	State/Prov.	Zip/Postal Code

Signature (if under 18, a parent or guardian must sign)

Mail to the Harlequin Reader Service:
IN U.S.A.: P.O. Box 1867, Buffalo, NY 14240-1867
IN CANADA: P.O. Box 609, Fort Erie, Ontario L2A 5X3

Not valid for current subscribers to Harlequin® American Romance® books.

Want to try two free books from another line?
Call 1-800-873-8635 or visit www.morefreebooks.com.

* Terms and prices subject to change without notice. Prices do not include applicable taxes. N.Y. residents add applicable sales tax. Canadian residents will be charged applicable provincial taxes and GST. Offer not valid in Quebec. This offer is limited to one order per household. All orders subject to approval. Credit or debit balances in a customer's account(s) may be offset by any other outstanding balance owed by or to the customer. Please allow 4 to 6 weeks for delivery. Offer available while quantities last.

Your Privacy: Harlequin is committed to protecting your privacy. Our Privacy Policy is available online at www.eHarlequin.com or upon request from the Reader Service. From time to time we make our lists of customers available to reputable third parties who may have a product or service of interest to you. If you would prefer we not share your name and address, please check here. ☐

Help us get it right—We strive for accurate, respectful and relevant communications. To clarify or modify your communication preferences, visit us at www.ReaderService.com/consumerschoice.

Silhouette *Desire*

THE WESTMORELANDS

NEW YORK TIMES
bestselling author

BRENDA JACKSON

HOT WESTMORELAND NIGHTS

Ramsey Westmoreland knew better than to lust
after the hired help. But Chloe, the new cook,
was just so delectable. Though their affair was
growing steamier, Chloe's motives became
suspicious. And when he learned Chloe was
carrying his child this Westmoreland Rancher
had to choose between pride or duty.

Available March 2010 wherever books are sold.

Always Powerful, Passionate and Provocative.